MASSAGE & MURDER

A COZY SPA MYSTERY

JENN COWAN

CONTENTS

Copyright	v
Chapter 1	1
Chapter 2	10
Chapter 3	17
Chapter 4	25
Chapter 5	31
Chapter 6	38
Chapter 7	44
Chapter 8	52
Chapter 9	58
Chapter 10	66
Chapter 11	76
Chapter 12	85
Chapter 13	92
Chapter 14	102
Chapter 15	117
Chapter 16	125
Chapter 17	132
Chapter 18	138
Chapter 19	144
Chapter 20	153
Chapter 21	160
Chapter 22	169
A Note From The Author	179
About the Author	181
Other Books by the Author:	183

COPYRIGHT

Copyright © 2018 Jenn Cowan

This book is a work of fiction. Names, characters, businesses, organizations, places, events, and incidents either are the product of the author's imagination or are used fictitiously. Any resemblance to actual person's, living or dead, events, or locales is entirely coincidental.

All rights reserved. No part of this publication may be reproduced, stored in a retrieval system, or transmitted, in any form or by any means, electronic, mechanical, photocopying, recording, or otherwise, without the prior permission of author.

1

Someone is trying to break into the spa. A person in a black hoodie is rattling the back door. It's ten a.m.; the spa is open. Why are they trying to get in the back door? The sign clearly states, Employee's Only.

I lock my jeep without clicking the alarm in order to not draw attention to myself. The thought of locking my jeep never occurs to me in the small town of Daysville. There's never any crime. We had a few broken windows from bored high schoolers over the past few months, but otherwise our town is crime free.

Snow starts to fall around me and the bitter wind is biting my cheeks. I can smell wood burning probably from the fireplace in the spa. I'm tempted to call out to this person, after all this is Daysville. Everyone knows everyone and if someone needs help, you help them, but something in my gut tells me to just watch. So, I do.

The person is medium height and medium build although I can't be too sure as they may be wearing layers. I can hear the scraping of metal like they're trying to pick the lock. What are they doing?

Someone blares a car horn in the parking lot next door. The person jumps and glances around. Their face is covered with a black ski mask. They see me and take off.

"Hey!" I call out hurrying toward them. My boots slap across the pavement then slip on a patch of ice and before I know it, I'm on my backside. Pain shoots down my hip, but I catch a glimpse of the SUV as it peels out of the parking lot. It's black with out of state plates. Which state I can't be sure, but it's not a Missouri plate. The numbers are blurry; I really need glasses.

I reach for my phone and dial the police station. Debra's pitchy voice greets me. "Debra, it's Autumn. Someone was trying to break into the spa."

"You're kidding!" she gasps as if this is the most shocking thing she's ever heard, which it probably is. Jaywalking and speeding are our biggest crimes.

"No, I'm not. They're driving a black SUV. Out of state plates, but I didn't catch the license number."

"I'll send someone right over."

"Thank you." I hang up, brush myself off and limp into the spa. What a way to start a Monday. I slip my key in the lock, it sticks, but only for a moment. Once it turns, I hurry into the spa making sure it's shut and locked behind me.

A familiar whiny voice floats into the employee break room. "I've been waiting ten minutes for a massage. The sign says, Walk-in's Welcome, is that not the case?"

I envision April with her blond bob, Barbie type body and designer suit pointing to the green sign with bold black letters on the door to the spa. A heel claps on the tile floor. More ranting ensues. I sigh and hang my wool coat on the rack next to the door. Static from my scarf causes my copper colored ponytail to spark like a lighter out of fluid. I straighten my black scrubs and stomp my black boots one more time on the Welcome rug to ensure all the snow is off. My hip still hurts so I limp toward the medicine cabinet and scrounge for the Arnica Cream. It's my miracle cream for all bruises and sore muscles. I slather it on and place it back in the cabinet.

"What happened to you?"

I jump and spin around, not realizing anyone else was in the breakroom. "Oh, hi Sally. I fell on the ice. Someone was trying to break in. Did you hear or see anything?"

Sally glances out the window. "I just sat down before you came in. I only heard your keys." She shrugs and goes back to flipping through her magazine like someone breaking into the spa is no big deal. Of course, she is from Chicago so maybe this sort of thing happens all the time in her neck of the woods.

I sigh and scoop up my blue "Breathe" tea mug from the dish rack then plop in two bags of chamomile tea before filling it with hot water from the tea kettle on the stove. I let the herbs fill my senses. Peaceful. Calming. Isn't that what a spa is supposed to be? Not when April graces us with her presence. I can still hear her whining.

April Biggs.

Ex-beauty queen.

Blond, busty and beautiful.

The town's queen bee.

Well, in her eyes. In everyone else's she's a pain in the... well let's just say we tolerate her. Why? Because it's what we do. Our little town of Daysville, MO is full of Southern charm although we're not really Southerners. We're at the tip of Missouri almost in Arkansas so we're close, right?

Anyway, we always smile. Use our manners. Never gossip on Sundays and pretend we love April Biggs.

Why?

Because her family runs this town.

Her grandfather was Mayor before he died last year of a heart attack. Now, her father is the Mayor. Her grandmother and mother have since passed. Cancer. God Rest Their Souls. They were staples in the community. Volunteering at the hospital, organizing fundraisers, supporting various charities and ensuring everyone knew the latest gossip.

April has taken their place only with less class, and way less grace. She tries, but she doesn't hold a candle to them. Her husband owns pretty much every building in town except for this spa. Not that he hasn't tried to buy out Vicky.

Vicky's my boss. She's a stubborn spitfire of a woman. Determined to pass the spa onto her daughter, Bethany.

Speaking of Bethany, I can hear her typing away on the computer, trying to re-arrange appointments to fit April into the schedule. "Sally is available now, but you requested another therapist."

I sneak a peek at Sally slouched on the plaid couch pretending to read the latest tabloid gossip. Her black hair is pulled back into a bun at the base of her neck and her black scrubs are practically hanging off her. Dark circles rim her brown eyes and stand out against her pale skin. She reminds me of a vampire except her teeth are perfect. Not a sharp tooth in sight. She sighs and tosses the magazine on the coffee table when April's voices screeches from the front, "You bet I want another therapist. That girl shouldn't have wasted her money on massage school. She massages like she's fluffing hair. Should have been a hairdresser instead of a massage therapist."

I cringe. April isn't wrong, but does she have to be so blunt...so rude? Wait, it's April, of course she does.

I open my mouth to say something encouraging to Sally when I hear my name.

"Autumn has a client at eleven, but usually comes in early. I'm sure she can work you in."

Guess that's my cue.

"I don't have time to wait. My schedule is packed today. I simply want someone to work out this kink in my neck before the ladies luncheon this afternoon."

"We just opened so Sally and Josh are our only two therapists here. Josh just went in with someone so unless you want Sally, you'll have to wait for Autumn." I hear Bethany sigh. Envision her flipping her brown braid over her shoulder. It's what she does when she's frustrated. "We do have some openings this afternoon if you would like me to schedule you after your luncheon."

Another sigh. This time from April. "If Walk-ins aren't available then you should take down the sign until they are available. It's bad business. Either hire more therapists, BETTER therapists or don't advertise for walk-ins." Nails tap on the counter then another sigh. "Someone should open another spa. Daysville is growing." Silence hangs like dark thunder clouds before the storm. "Maybe that should be my new business venture."

I hear a click, probably April opening her expensive hand bag. Another clap. Heels clicking along the tile floor. "Bobby. I know what I want to do for our next building project." A jingle of the bell over the spa door, a blast of cold air then silence. Bethany must have pointed to the 'No Cell Phone' sign. At least now the spa's quiet.

I cast a glance back to Sally only she's disappeared. The bathroom door is shut, and I hear soft whimpers from behind the door.

I'm torn.

Comfort Sally or save Bethany?

I start toward the bathroom.

"Oh, Autumn. Thank goodness. Mrs. Biggs is here demanding a massage from anyone other than Sally." She glances around then rolls her eyes.

I smile, press a finger to my lips and gesture toward the bathroom. "I think I can fit her in. Also, a detective should be by soon. Someone was trying to break into the spa."

Bethany gasps. "Break in? When?"

"A couple of minutes ago. I saw them when I pulled up. Someone honked, they saw me and took off. I slipped on the ice chasing them." I rub my hip.

"Oh no! Are you ok?" Bethany touches my arm.

"Nothing a little Arnica cream can't fix."

"That stuff is amazing. Used it right after I hit my leg on the coffee table and didn't even get a bruise.'"

The bell chimes out front.

"She's back," Bethany groans and hands me April's file.

I glance back at the bathroom door. The whimpering's stopped. Maybe Sally just needs some space. I can catch up with her over lunch although the girl barely says more than a couple of sentences to anyone.

My boots squeak against the tile floor. I slow my pace and stand on my tiptoes as I pass the Green room even though it's not necessary. These walls are practically sound proof. Perfect to ensure client confidentiality. Since the door is closed, Josh must be with a client.

Josh Parker is my best friend. He's also my neighbor. We've lived next door to each other since we were born. Our parents are best friends hence we're best friends. When our parents retired to Florida they sold us their houses. Well, actually they gave us their houses.

His house is a bright blue and mine, a bright yellow. We joke that I'm the sun and he's my sky. The metaphor isn't wrong. I'm the social butterfly; usually the center of everything while he hangs around ensuring no one messes with me.

He's my dream guy. Dark hair, blue eyes, athletic build, tall but not towering and boy, can the guy give an incredible massage. A muffled moan from behind the door seconds that. We went to massage school right out of high school. He wanted to transition into physical therapy and work with athletes, but decided against it for some unknown reason he refuses to share with me...his best friend.

Am I bitter?

Maybe.

Anyway, in massage school the girls swooned. Even some of the guys. Between his pretty boy good looks and his hands, which are strong, magical and healing, he's nearly perfect.

Why just nearly perfect?

Because there's no spark. No fire. He's like my brother. Always teasing me. Making me smell his armpit. He's also extremely quiet and shy in public. Around me, he won't stop talking, but he hates crowds. Hates socializing. Would rather stay home and read a book than go to a football game. We're so opposite it's painful. Except when it comes to massage.

Massage is the one thing we have in common. We love everything about it, how everything in the body is connected. It's like a map and we're the navigators. This muscle connects to this one and this point corresponds to this organ. It's all so interesting and rewarding.

We heal people. Make them feel better. Help them relax. Forget the world. Forget their problems. Give them a safe space to just be. To breathe. Hence my tea cup. I take another sip letting the chamomile calm my nerves and brace myself for April. Did I mention she's my mortal enemy?

"Oh, Autumn." She rolls her eyes and wrinkles her nose as if I smell. I turn my head and sniff just in case. Lavender and vanilla. My favorite lotion. She must be snarling at the thought of me touching her. Josh usually works on her, but he's busy. Sally isn't good enough so I guess she's stuck with me. Believe me, I'm not very excited about it either. She sighs. "Can you fit me in?" she mutters.

I nod. Keeping my face expressionless and stoic. I'm a professional. I can do this.

She sighs again. "The women's luncheon is in an hour, so I only have about thirty minutes and my neck's killing me. Just be sure not to mess up my hair. You do have a towel or a cap to keep oil from getting in it, don't you?" April pats her blond bob.

"Of course." I grit my teeth and plaster on a smile. "We'll be in the blue room." I escort her down the long hallway and hold open the last door on the right. "Remove as much clothing as you're comfortable with and please remove your jewelry. I will have you start face down and—

April waves me off. "I know the drill. Don't go far. I'll be ready in a minute."

I fight the urge to roll my eyes and close the door behind her still gritting my teeth. My jaw starts to ache, so I take a deep breath and set down my tea mug before making a note in April's chart. I walk back toward the reception area to snag a couple of heat packs. I overhear Bethany on the phone. She must be talking to her mom because she sounds upset.

"Mrs. Biggs is going to open another spa. She was just talking about it with her husband. It's going to be their new project. Daysville can't support two spas. They'll sink us. With all their money, we won't have a chance."

I'm straining to hear what else she's saying to her mother when Sally comes out of the bathroom.

Her eyes are puffy and her nose is red. She spots the heat packs in my hands and asks, "Working on the ice queen?"

I smirk and nod.

"Good luck," she says before heading back into the break room.

I'll need it.

2

I head back down the hall, slip into the blue room and adjust the sheets. A half an hour massage is never long enough. It's a spot massage, so I'll focus solely on April's neck and pray I don't strangle her.

Just kidding.

I'm a professional.

Mortal enemies or not.

I place a hair wrap around her bob and set the heat packs on her back and neck.

The silence is awkward and heavy. Luckily, massage sessions are usually quiet so we don't have to talk. Nor do I want too.

I place a pillow underneath her ankles.

April's grating voice startles me. "I'm going to open a new spa across town." She turns her head and rests her cheek on the face rest.

I almost groan out loud. Talking to April is something I avoid at all costs. It's too painful. Too emotional. Too traumatizing. It's been fifteen years. I should be over it. I am over it. I straighten my shoulders, take a deep breath and force myself to ask, "Really? Why?"

April huffs and waves her hand. "Vicky's Spa is a joke. I mean I had to wait until you came in to get a massage. She shouldn't advertise for walk-ins if therapists aren't available."

"Sally was available," I say through gritted teeth as I oil my hands and knead her feet.

She snorts. "That girl is awful. She should have never become a massage therapist."

I dig deeply into the sole of her foot.

"A little too much, Autumn," she gasps.

I reduce my pressure, smile and apologize although secretly it gave me great satisfaction. When April doesn't say anything else I spend a few more minutes on her feet before sanitizing my hands and moving to her back and neck.

April sighs and says, "Don't you think Vicky's Spa is outdated?" She doesn't give me time to answer before continuing, "I mean the décor out front...yuck. White walls, plaid couches and green tile." April shutters. "I've been to spas in New York and they're so modern. Clean lines. Leather couches. Water features. Soft music playing throughout the spa not just in the treatment rooms. Spring water with cucumbers. Facials, body wraps, pedicures, manicures."

"We have all those services."

April nods. "The same services. Nothing new. Vicky hasn't changed her menu or the decor in years. This room is so blue. Blue walls. Blue sheets. Blue rug. Blue chair. I wouldn't be surprised if the massage table itself were blue. I mean I'm all for themes, but this is ridiculous."

I glance around the room at the worn carpet, chipping paint and frayed rug. The heat packs are continuously being patched when rice starts to fall out of them and the hot towel cabi and electric blankets are on their last legs. Some days they work and others they don't. Vicky does need to update things a bit, but I wasn't about to agree with April.

"I mean how many seaweed wraps can one person do? Where's the mud wraps? The cellulite treatments? There's no variety. And don't get me started on her facials. They're so basic. Cleanser, exfoliator, mud mask, toner, moisturizer. Everything is the same. The woman could afford to branch out with the rates she charges. Even try some new services. The spa in New York has a steaming service that opens your pores. It feels like a shower for my face. The massages are different too. Different oils and aromas used in each service. Different techniques. More therapists. They didn't have any trouble getting me in on short notice although the Biggs name does have some clout in New York. I think it's time Daysville gets an elite spa. Something unique and sophisticated. Don't you agree?"

I don't answer as I press an elbow into April's shoulder.

She moans. "Oh, that's the spot."

Thankfully, she quits talking and turns to put her face back in the face rest.

After a few minutes, I ask, "Is that too much pressure?" I'm probably using too much.

"Goodness, no. So much better than Sally although not as good as Josh. I will be recruiting him for my new spa."

I apply more pressure because the thought of Josh working for her makes my blood boil.

"Oh, a little too much," she complains.

I back off and take a breath. I need to chill out. Put my history with April aside and do my job.

Moments later soft snores drift from beneath the face rest.

I sigh and watch the clock minutes tick by as I move around working on April's neck and upper back. Thirty minutes feels like ninety, but it's finally over. "Take your time and I'll meet you out front." I whisper.

April snorts and mumbles something I can't make out.

I won't be surprised if she falls back asleep. Her breathing is deep and she's completely relaxed. Not as good as Josh, my eye. I snag her file and step from the room, closing the door softly behind me.

Vicky's voice floats down the hallway. "Over my dead body will she open another spa in this town."

Jotting down a few notes, I make my way to the mini fridge behind the reception area. I snag a bottle of water and set it on the counter for April. Hydration is key after a massage. Prevents clients from being sore. A massage is like a workout. The day after most clients can be sore. Drinking water tends to reduce it.

"Did April say anything to you about opening a spa?" Vicky places a hand on her wide hip. Her black scrubs are clinging to her curvy frame and she's glaring at me with the 'mom look'. I hate that look. Her curly brown hair frames her face. Red rimmed glasses are perched on her thin nose and her brown eyes are narrowed, practically scorching me with their intensity.

I hand April's file to Bethany and fill out my therapist log to track my hours, but really, I'm buying time because she's not going to like what I have to say. I take a deep breath and face her. "You know I can't talk about what my clients discuss during their massage."

Vicky makes a face and stomps from the room.

"Mom is livid," Bethany whispers, flipping her braid over her shoulder before she tugs on her black scrub top to hide her curves. She's the spitting image of her mother only with long brown hair, which she always braids and she wears contacts in her brown eyes as opposed to glasses.

"I can tell." I check the schedule then glance around the waiting room. "Did a detective show up?"

Bethany nods and shifts back and forth, avoiding eye contact. "He's waiting in the break room for you. Nikki showed up early so I put her in the yellow room with some heat packs on her back. That way we can avoid any issues."

"Issues?" I raise an eyebrow.

"You didn't hear?"

I shake my head.

"She and April had an argument the other night during the garden club," Bethany whispers, glancing toward the door.

I gasp and lean in closer so April doesn't hear us when she comes out, but before I can get any more details, Regina Mills, the owner of Regina's Hair Salon next door, waltzes in. Bringing in a blast of cold air and some snow.

"Did they see each other?" Regina brushes the snow off her dyed red hair then smacks her gum before tucking a comb into her smock. "I have a client waiting, but didn't want to miss the fireworks." Her blue eyes sparkling with mischief.

Bethany smirks and shakes her head. "No fireworks here. This is a spa not a grandstand."

Regina waves a wrinkled hand at her. "With the farmer's almanac predicting snow until the end of March these are all the fireworks we're going to see for a while. These two have been lighting each other's fuses since middle school. Especially when April stole Bobby from Nikki during their senior year in high school." She blows a bubble and sucks it in with a pop.

"Oh, I almost forgot about that." Bethany sets her elbows

on the desk and props her chin on her hands. Giving Regina her full attention.

"Well you were only six when it happened over fifteen years ago. Autumn, you remember, don't you?" She pauses and studies me. I feel like a microorganism under a microscope. "Of course, you do. Bobby isn't the only guy April stole from her 'best friends'." Regina pursues her lips and gives me a pointed look.

I feel my face flush. I know what she's referring too, but there's no way I'm re-hashing high school with the aunt of the love of my life.

"Anyway, Bobby was the love of Nikki's life. No man has ever been good enough for her. It's sad really. She's so pretty. All that raven hair. Silky loose curls. I love styling her hair." Regina sighs and stares off into space for a moment as if dreaming about Nikki's hair then snaps backs to reality and says, "Not to mention, she's beautiful inside and out. Not like that witch April." Regina makes a face. She's never been an April fan. Although after what April did to her nephew, I can't say I blame her. I do blame him though, and of course, April. Regina's gum smacking brings me back to the present. "Speaking of the witch. Where is she?"

I glance at the clock. It's been almost ten minutes. "I'll go check on her. She may have fallen back asleep."

"You do have magical hands." Regina winks at me before popping another bubble.

I give her a genuine smile then head to the blue room. Hopefully she's dressed and just checking her make-up. I hate waking up clients. They're always groggy and usually embarrassed about falling back asleep. I lift my hand and rap softly on the door. "April." I call out softly.

No answer.

I knock a little louder. "April. It's 10:45."

Nothing.

I knock again.

Still nothing. That's strange. She must really be asleep.

"April, I'm coming in."

I peek in the room and freeze. My heart drops and I have the urge to throw up. I force myself to hold it together as I yell, "Bethany! Call an ambulance NOW!"

3

"Autumn?"

I jump and nearly spill my tea on my scrubs. My feet are tucked underneath me and I'm snuggled underneath a soft blanket Bethany wrapped around me when I couldn't stop shaking. I've been sitting in the break room staring at the wall for the past ten minutes after finding her.

I can't erase the image of April face down on the massage table with a knife sticking out of her back. Blood soaking the blue sheets. There's not enough bleach in the world to get all that blood out. I don't think I'll ever be able to give a massage in that room again. I blink and turn toward the voice. All thoughts of April disappear. My heart betrays me and starts a stampede in my chest as I take in the man who broke my heart fifteen years ago.

Travis Mills.

The complete opposite of my dream guy...at least in the looks department.

Red crew cut. Green eyes. Tall, toweringly tall. In high school, he was buff now he's annoyingly ripped. Ugh. Does the man have to wear a shirt that tight? I mean I can see his pecs through his white dress shirt and that suit. Dark like his mood and his red tie...the color of well I won't go there. My mouth goes dry.

This is the man who owned my heart. He gets me...or he did. We like the same things or at least we did in high school. In high school, we were the 'it' couple. Life's of the party, always laughing, always having fun. We understood each other. Supported each other. Loved each other. Even now, I'm so drawn to him I can't stand it. Just looking at him has me wanting to throw myself at him and forgive his mistake.

Except I can't.

He's a dad. The main reason we're not together. The big mistake that is now big...a fourteen-year old daughter, Catherine. Everyone calls her Cat. She's a sweetheart unlike her mother.

Her mother, April.

Yeah. Now, you see why she's my mortal enemy?

My dead mortal enemy.

I shudder.

I know you shouldn't speak ill of the dead, but well...she stole my boyfriend, got pregnant then dumped him and stole Bobby from Nikki.

Two guys, a red-haired baby and a paternity test proved Travis was the father. Although the red hair was probably enough to prove Travis was the father. Bobby has dark brown hair and there's never been a red head in his family, but April wanted to make sure. She cried when she found out, because she was positive Bobby was the father. She and Bobby were already married because she told him the baby was his. He could have divorced her, but he didn't. I'll never understand why. So, they stayed married and Travis became a teenage dad, sharing custody with the wicked witch of Daysville.

I'd feel sorry for him if he hadn't betrayed me. I mean we were taking a break. You know those breaks high schoolers take for like a weekend then by Monday realize they can't live without each other. Apparently, he could live without me. And I guess I could live without him because that's what I'm doing, right?

I'm living.

Not dating.

Not married.

No kids.

Content to spend my time at the spa, doing what I love, going out with my girlfriends or snuggling up on my couch binge watching Netflix with Josh. That's my life and I love it, but staring into those piercing green eyes I become a love-sick teenager all over again.

He's leaning against the door frame of the break room, looking like he just stepped out of a Men's Warehouse magazine.

The silence is like a ticking time bomb. Neither of us know what to say. We don't see each other even in this small town. It's like everyone runs interference for us. We rarely cross paths and when we do, it's like a punch in the gut. All those feelings. The love. The memories. The kisses. The pain. The betrayal. The hate. It's all rolled into one big emotional knitting ball. His aunt Regina could knit an entire army scarves with our history.

Travis clears his throat. He has a job to do. He's a detective. Although I'm surprised he's on this case since it's the mother of his child who was murdered. Maybe Captain Green figured he'd work twice as hard to find the killer since it's personal or Travis simply refused to be taken off the case.

My bet is on the latter. "Can you run me thru what happened?"

I sigh. No greeting. No small talk just right to the point. Sometimes I miss the old Travis. The one I would talk to for hours on the phone. Tell him my secrets, my hopes, my dreams. This Travis is cold. Shut down. Unfriendly and obviously wanting to get this interview over with as soon as possible. Well me too. "I gave MRS. BIGGS a thirty-minute massage." Emphasis on the Mrs. Biggs part. It's petty I know. Old wounds are starting to crack open. Bitterness is rising in my throat, ready to spill out. I tap it down and continue, "I stepped out to give her time to get dressed. When she didn't come out, I went to check on her and found her." I run a hand down my ponytail then toy with the end. The memory of April lying on the table with a knife in her back would be forever burned in my mind.

"How long was it before you went to check on her?"

"Ten minutes or so."

He frowns. "Do you usually wait that long to check on clients?"

I narrow my eyes at him. "Usually my clients come right out within a couple of minutes. I was talking to Bethany and your aunt and lost track of time." I pause. "Like I said, usually my clients come right out."

He nods and jots something down in his mini notepad. "Did you and April talk about anything?"

"We did."

"What did you talk about?"

I wrap my hands around my mug. "I can't tell you."

"Why not?"

"Client confidentiality."

"The client is dead."

I shrug.

"Don't make this any harder, Autumn."

I jut out my chin before taking a sip of my tea.

His eyes darken and I can see him working his jaw. Clenching and unclenching it. He's getting angry. Oh, well. I'm not losing my license over this. "I'll get a warrant," he threatens.

I shrug again.

"Don't make me arrest you, Autumn." His voice low and gruff.

I scoff. "For what?"

"The list is growing, but right now you are the last person to see April alive. You're our primary suspect. You have means, motive and opportunity."

My jaw drops. "Means?"

"You're capable of killing April. Have access to the kitchen knife we found in her back." He gestures with his pen to the taped off area where the knife block sits on the counter, the biggest knife slot is empty. A young blond-haired officer is guarding it as if it's the most important job ever. "It matches the other knives in the set."

"That means nothing. Anyone could access those knives."

He gives me a pointed look. "You also have motive."

"What motive?"

He gestures back and forth between us.

"You?" I almost laugh. "You're my motive? That's ridiculous." I take another sip of tea, but my hands are shaking so much I almost miss my mouth.

"So, you're not still upset about what happened in high school."

"That was fifteen years ago. I've moved on."

"Have you?"

"Don't flatter yourself. I haven't spent the last fifteen

years pining for you. Believe me, I'm totally over it," I smile as I lie through my teeth and pray he buys it.

He studies me for a moment before moving on, "You also had opportunity. Thirty minutes of opportunity. Stab April. Slip out like nothing happened then when she doesn't come out, make a show of finding her body."

I almost let go of my mug. Tea splashes over the rim and burns my hand, but I barely feel it. He's really making a case against me. The room is spinning or am I spinning? I can't tell. This can't be happening. I feel sick. Sure, I hate April...hated her. Envisioned killing her multiple times, but I would never do it. Would never leave Cat without a mother. I'm not a killer. I'm a healer. Surely, Travis knows that. I glance up at him as he's reviewing his notes...then again maybe he doesn't.

Bethany pokes her head in the room. "Autumn, you're as white as snow. Are you alright?"

I shake my head. "I'm feeling kind of sick." My hands are shaking. Tea is threatening to spill from my cup again and I want to vomit. Preferably on Travis's shiny black dress shoes.

"Autumn," Josh pushes past Bethany and Travis, who scowls at him and pulls me into his strong arms. "How are you holding up?"

I inhale him. His shampoo is a mixture of tea tree and mint. It's an odd combo, but it works and it's totally him. I start to cry. I'm not a crier, but suddenly my emotions are all over the place. Between seeing April, working on April, finding her dead on my massage table and having an emotional stand-off with my ex, my emotions are shot.

"Let's get you home," Josh whispers in my ear.

I nod into his chest, letting him pull me to my feet. Leaning against him for support.

"I'm not done questioning her." Travis puffs out his chest and blocks Josh from retrieving our coats.

Josh stiffens. His voice gruff and commanding. "You're done for now. Any further questions will happen at the police station with Autumn's lawyer present."

My lawyer? I don't have a lawyer. The only lawyer in town is Miss Waters and she's not very good. Josh has to be joking. I didn't do anything wrong. There's no need for a lawyer. I glance up at the two men. They're having a stare down. I roll my eyes. This is like high school all over again.

Josh never thought Travis was good enough for me and repeatedly told him so. When things went south and April got pregnant, Josh did the unthinkable…he punched Travis right in his perfectly straight nose, which now isn't so straight. In fact, it's looking rather crooked these days.

Travis deserved it. If my eyes hadn't been puffy and swollen from crying so much and I had the desire to stop watching Full House re-runs while making my way through five cartons of mint chocolate chip ice cream, I probably would have punched him too…only not in the eye.

I squeeze Josh's waist to remind him I'm still here and he squeezes back.

"Excuse us. We need to get our coats."

Someone calls Travis's name from down the hall. He glares at Josh before his eyes land on me. They soften slightly before he hands me his business card. "Call me when you've secured a lawyer and we'll talk." Then he stomps from the room.

A whimper escapes me.

Josh gives me another squeeze. "He's just trying to intimidate you. We'll call your father when we get to your house. Once the snow stops, I'm sure he'll drive in to represent you."

My father? Oh right. My father. Retired attorney. Although, he still works part time much to my mother's despair. After his heart attack two years ago, she forced him to retire to Florida. Now, he spends his days playing golf and chugging fresh squeezed juice my mother forces down his throat with an array of various vitamins and supplements to keep him healthy. I shake my head. Never in a million years did I think my dad would be representing me. Could this day get any worse?

A scream and angry voices come from the waiting room.

Apparently, it could.

4

Josh and I exchange a curious look, forget our coats and head toward the waiting room. We step into the waiting room to find Bobby Biggs lunging for Travis. Travis pushes his daughter, Cat out of the way. She staggers and falls back onto the plaid couch. I rush to her side and move her behind the reception desk.

Josh tries to separate the two men, but between the shouting and the flying fists, he's struggling. It's like watching two football players fighting with the ref trying to break them up. Someone is bound to end up hurt. I glance around for help. Where are all the officers? This is a crime scene.

As if reading my mind, two officers come rushing in and try to restrain Bobby while Josh and another officer try to hold onto Travis. I let out the breath I've been holding. The shouting continues, but at least no fists are flying.

I ignore the men, even though I'm curious what they're fighting about, and focus on Cat. She's shaking beside me; my heart breaks for her. The girl just lost her mother and the two fathers in her life are acting like a bunch of teenage jocks. Men. I shake my head in disgust.

Her short red hair is sticking to her freckled face. Tears are about to spill from her green eyes. Eyes she got from her father. I glance at Travis. His suit is wrinkled and his face is red. Blood drips from his nose. I sneak a peek at Bobby. The bulky guy is bleeding from his lip onto his wrinkled dark suit and striped tie. His left eye is turning black and his short brown hair is sticking up in all directions like he just rolled out of bed.

A whimper beside me pulls me back to Cat.

"Let's get you something warm to drink."

She nods and stands. I place my arm around her shoulder and guide her back toward the break room. She starts to cry again, which only makes my heart ache even more. The poor girl must be devastated over her mother's death. I glance down the hall and shudder when I see the yellow and black crime scene tape across the door to the blue room. An image of April flashes through my mind and I force it away. Cat needs me. I can dwell on everything else later.

I steer her toward the couch and motion for her to sit before hurrying to prepare her something to drink. "Tea, okay?"

"Chamomile," she whispers.

I smile. A girl after my own heart. "It's my favorite."

She gives me a small smile. "Mine too. Mom hates it...hated it."

I cringe and try not to roll my eyes at the same time as I prepare the tea. The blond officer is watching me closely. Probably afraid I will taint the evidence. I ignore him and say, "Not everyone can appreciate the flavor or the benefits." I bite my lip, hoping that didn't sound rude.

"That's exactly what I say."

I beam. I can't help it. This girl is more like her father than her mother. Thank the good Lord for that. I hand her the tea mug that says Relax, which seems fitting for the situation. "I'm so sorry about your mother."

Cat wraps her bony hands around the mug. "She had it coming."

"What?" I try to keep my voice level, but her words catch me off guard. I glance at the officer, but he's checking something on his phone. So much for diligence.

"No one in town likes her. Everyone smiles to her face then talks about her behind her back. Well at least they did." She takes a sip of tea.

I'm not sure what to say. Lying doesn't seem to be an option. The girl obviously has things figured out. "Cat, do you know who might want to hurt your mom?"

Cat shrugs. "Everyone."

Huh. Smart girl. "Has your mom had any issues with anyone lately?"

"Half the town. She was always lighting fires and Bobby put them out. It's what they did. Why they worked."

This girl was wise beyond her years.

"Bobby thinks my dad killed my mom. That's why they're fighting," Cat whispers, eyeing the police officer, who is scrolling through his phone.

My mouth drops open. "Your dad wasn't even here when your mother...well when it happened."

Cat gives me a look. "He was here."

"He was?"

"We were having breakfast since this is the last day of Christmas break. He got a call from the station. You reported an attempted break in. He's the only detective on duty since the other two are on vacation." Cat takes another sip of tea. Her hands shaking slightly.

"Did you come with him?"

"I was waiting in the car. He didn't think he'd be long. Then I saw the ambulance and several police cars so I came inside to see what was going on. No one would tell me anything. Just told me to sit on the couch and wait for my dad. I thought it was protocol. Contain the scene. Protect the victim. That sort of thing. I just figured someone slipped and hit their head or something. I didn't think someone was..." She took another sip of tea. "Then Bobby showed up and I knew something happened to mom. She was complaining all weekend about her neck and I saw her SUV in the parking lot so I knew she was here." She sniffles.

"Why does Bobby think your dad hurt your mom?"

"Don't answer that," Travis barks, stomping into the room. "Let's go, Cat." He holds out a hand to help her up.

"I want to finish my tea." She lifts her mug as if showing proof.

"It's time to go."

Cat opens her mouth to protest, but I cut her off. "Take the mug. We have plenty."

"Are you sure?" She glances down at the mug and runs a slender finger over the words.

"Positive." I pat her arm and smile.

"Thank you," she whispers and returns the smile before standing up next to her dad.

I didn't realize how tall she was until she stood next to Travis. She came up to his shoulder and was his mini me. "You're welcome." I stand felling incredibly short in their presence. "Please let me know if there is anything I can do." I keep my eyes focused on Cat, but can feel Travis's eyes on me.

Cat nods and lets her father guide her from the room.

I watch them leave then stifle a smile when I see him and Josh sizing each other up as they pass each other in the hall.

Josh glares after Travis before turning his attention to me. "It's not even noon and this place is like a three-ring circus."

I shake my head. "Are you alright?" I take in a bruise forming on his cheek.

He shrugs and heads to the stove, ignoring the officer, who seems to have forgotten his duty to contain the scene and has resorted to texting. Josh pours himself some tea while I pull the Arnica cream from the medicine cabinet. When he collapses on the couch, I slather his cheek with the cream. He hisses at me, but I ignore him. "Hopefully, it won't bruise too badly." I replace the cap, toss the cream on the coffee table and lean my head back on the couch. "Can you believe April Biggs is dead? It seems like a bad dream."

Josh pinches me.

"Hey! What was that for?" I rub my forearm.

"Waking us up if we're dreaming." He smirks.

I swat his arm. "Not funny."

"Who's laughing?" His face appears innocent, but I can see the gleam in his eyes.

I roll my eyes then rest my head on his shoulder. "Did you get any details on the fight?"

Josh sighs. "Apparently, April was wanting to ship Cat off to boarding school and Travis was fighting her on it. They were about to go to court over it."

"Why would April want to send Cat to boarding school?"

Josh shrugs. "Only thing I caught over all the yelling was it was a prestigious girls school and looks good on college resumes."

I scowl. "April was always about what looks good on paper."

"That she was." He takes another sip of tea. "I'm starving. What did you bring us for lunch?"

"How can you think of food when someone was just murdered?" I shift so he can get up.

"I'm a guy. We can always eat." He heads to the fridge and pulls out the Tupperware filled with salad and grilled chicken. "Want some?"

I hold up my hand and fight the urge to gag. He sits back down and digs in while I think about what Cat told me. Everyone in town has a motive to kill April, but who actually did? It's the billion-dollar question, one I have to prove before Travis decides to pin the murder on me. Not to mention he never asked me about the attempted break-in. Was that person trying to break-in to kill April or was there another reason?

5

I shift in the wooden pew. My wool coat is practically suffocating me even though it's freezing outside. Josh arches an eyebrow at me. My face is flushed; I can feel it. My vision blurs; I may pass out. If we weren't jammed into the middle of the pew, I would slip out and escape into the fresh air. The church smells of candlewax and Pine-sol. I grab a pamphlet and fan myself. How much longer can Preacher John keep talking? He's said practically the same thing three times.

"Are you ok?" Josh whispers in my ear.

I nod.

"Then quit fidgeting."

I wish I could. I hate funerals. Have since my grandfather died. I threw up in the middle of the aisle when I saw his stiff body. Of course, I was only five at the time. My stomach flips at the memory. I hate dead bodies. Live ones are fine, but dead ones not so much, especially when I'm being accused of killing the deceased.

April is on display in a shiny coffin with a silk lining. Dressed in a red suit and silky white blouse, her blond hair frames her face and her make-up is picture perfect. She looks like sleeping beauty. Only she's not. She's dead and someone here killed her.

I glance around the small church. It's a sea of black. The town of Daysville wears black to funerals. Not gray. Not brown. Just black. It's a sign of respect. A sign of mourning. At least that's what my mother told me when I threw a tantrum about having to wear a black dress to my grandfather's funeral.

Now, black is one of my favorite colors. Although I only wear this black dress to funerals. It reeks of death and hangs in the back of my closet until someone dies. I had to have it dry cleaned because it's been over a year since old man Wyatt passed away at the ripe old age of one hundred and two. That's what happens in Daysville. People die of old age, they're not murdered.

I shiver at the thought. A murderer is among us. It doesn't make sense. Who would kill April? Sure, everyone wanted to, but to really kill her, who would do that? And why?

I spot Bethany and Vicky sitting a couple rows in front of me. They're whispering back and forth. I pursue my lips. Vicky left the reception desk shortly after I came out. April was planning to open another spa in town which could have put Vicky out of business. Maybe I will add my boss to the suspect list.

Suspect list?

Yes, I'm creating one.

Why?

Because my ex-boyfriend thinks I killed the mother of his child in some sort of sick revenge for something that happened over fifteen years ago. Does he really think I would hold a grudge that long? Ok so I have, but still, I didn't kill her.

I can see the top of Travis's head. His red hair sticks out in the first pew along with his daughter's and his aunt's. They're a red-headed trio. Cat is sitting next to her dad. She's sniffling and her red hair is falling around her face. Regina is on the other side of her with an arm wrapped around her slender shoulder.

Bobby and the Mayor are across the aisle in the other first pew. Both men are dressed in dark suits and look stoic.

The rumor pool has been swirling since the murder. Some people in town suspect me. Mrs. Wright with her squinty eyes and wide rimmed glasses shoots me an evil look. I smile and nod. She scoffs and turns away. That's right, I will not be bullied by these people. Most of them have known me since I was in diapers. I'm not a killer. I'm a healer.

I spot Nikki sitting two rows behind Bobby. Her green eyes are glued to the back of his head. She's the complete opposite of April. Long black hair falls in loose curls down her back, olive skin glows in the candle light and her black dress clings to her petite yet toned body. There's nothing fake about her. She owns the Yoga studio in town and spends her spare time volunteering at the soup kitchen and in the children's wing of the hospital. Why Bobby chose April over her is another mystery. Could she have killed April? Much like me she was at the spa and has means and motive.

April stole the love of her life. Although Bobby never had a child with April, he did marry her. Not that Bobby didn't want a child, he did, but years of trying led to no children so everyone was convinced he couldn't have any. Bobby and April traded more children for businesses. They began taking over Daysville. The businesses became their children and of course, Cat. They all seemed to get along so why was April planning to send Cat away to school? It didn't make sense.

I glance at Travis again. I better put him on the suspect list too. He was at the spa, in the break room where he had access to the knife and he has a motive to kill April. If someone was going to send my daughter away, I would probably kill them too. Travis didn't have the money to fight April in court. Regina always talks about how he pays a lot in child support even though April is loaded. It never made sense to me, although I'll never understand custody situations. Court fees alone would probably break him. It may be a stretch to accuse Travis, but I can't rule anyone out, even a detective. My freedom and reputation depends on it. No one is going to want to get a massage from a suspected killer. The sooner I find out who killed April the better.

Movement by the back door catches my eye. Sally. She slips out letting in a blast of cold air. Where's she going? More importantly why is she here? She didn't really even know April. She's only been in town for a little over a month and every interaction she's had with April has been anything but pleasant.

Maybe I should add Sally to the list. April did insult her massage technique. Not a strong motive, but she did make the girl cry.

Sally moved to town about a month ago and hasn't made much of an effort to get to know very many people. She's quiet and withdrawn. There's a story there, but I can't seem to draw it out of her.

She's young. Maybe twenty. Lives alone in an apartment close to the spa. A building owned by Bobby and April.

Hmm. Maybe she has more motive than I thought. Eviction? I saw her last paycheck. It was barely enough to cover groceries let alone rent and utilities.

If the girl could just get more clients, she'd be fine. Massage therapists make a decent hourly wage. Of course, owning the spa is more profitable, but Josh and I aren't quite ready for that commitment. Not that we haven't discussed it, but we don't want to step on Vicky's toes. She pays us well and we don't have to worry about employees, overhead expenses, business licenses or other small business owner stuff.

We get to set our own schedules. Work and go home. It's a pretty sweet deal. Except when you don't have clients...like Sally. Most days she sits around the spa waiting for clients. Some days she works on one or two people and other days she just sits in the break room waiting for a walk-in. Bethany mentioned last week about letting her go, but since the spa has been closed the past four days for the investigation, I doubt she's been fired.

I need to talk to Sally. Get more of her story. I can't jump to conclusions. Facts. I need facts. All the good amateur sleuths do that, right? As soon as Preacher John is done droning on about April's accomplishments, I can try and find Sally.

Oh good, he's done.

We stand and pray. I bow my head and feel someone staring at me. I glance over to see Mary, the hospital director, staring at me. Her mousy face is pinched, brown eyes wide, curly salt and pepper hair smashed down by her black hat. She motions for me to come over to her. Everyone is filing out of the pews. I squeeze Josh's hand and nod toward Mary.

He follows my gaze and whispers, "I'll grab you a plate."

My hero. My stomach growls it's thanks. First stop, Mary

then I can eat. The Biggs are hosting a buffet in the town hall after the funeral. The burial is family only so everyone else gets to go eat.

I excuse my way through the crowd, but can't find Mary. Where did that mousy woman disappear too?

"Autumn."

The voice sends shivers down my spine. I turn around and come face to face with Travis. Cat is on his right so I focus on her. "I'm so sorry for your loss." I reach out and squeeze her hand. She squeezes back.

"Thank you. I have your mug. I can bring it by the spa tomorrow."

I open my mouth to tell her to keep it and the spa is currently closed when Travis says, "Cat, will you please go find your aunt? She went to the bathroom. We need to head to the cemetery."

Cat nods and let's go of my hand then shoots me a knowing look and disappears.

I stare after her. What was that about?

Travis clears his throat.

I tug on the strap of my purse and glare up at him.

He smirks. "The investigation at the spa was finished yesterday so you should be able to resume business tomorrow."

That's strange why didn't Vicky call me and let me know? I must have had a look on my face because Travis leans down and whispers, "That is if you still have a job."

I frown and fight the urge to stomp on his foot. "Why wouldn't I?"

"People don't want a massage from a murderer."

I gasp. "I would never hurt anyone let alone kill someone. You know me, Travis. I scoop up spiders and release them outside. Killing April? Why? Why now? If I wanted to kill her, why wouldn't I have killed her in high school?" I hiss.

Travis shrugs. "Some people just snap. Years of holding onto feelings."

I fume. "That's ridiculous. There's no feelings. I didn't kill April. Got it?" I poke his chest to get my point across.

He covers my finger with his hand. The touch sends a spark through my body. I quickly pull it out of his grasp.

"No feelings, huh?" He runs a hand through his hair. "You're a smart, independent and beautiful thirty-three-year old woman. You've never married. You hardly date. Unless..." he frowns and pursues his lips.

"Unless what?"

"You and Josh?"

"Josh?!" I shriek. A few people chatting in the back turn toward us. I lower my voice. "You think I'm dating Josh. My best friend, who let me remind you as I did in high school is like a brother to me."

"But he's not your brother."

I throw up my hands. "You're insane. This is like high school all over again. You always were jealous of Josh. I'm not dating Josh and I didn't kill April. Got it, detective?" I turn to leave.

Travis catches my arm. "I still am," he whispers in my ear.

I turn to face him. "Still are what?" Our faces are inches apart. I hold my breath.

"Jealous of Josh." Then he lets me go and waltzes out the door.

What the heck does that mean?

6

"Autumn! Are you alright?" Mary comes rushing up to me.

I nod not sure I can trust my voice yet. My heart is racing and my arm still burns from Travis's touch. Why does he still have an impact on me?

"You two can still heat up a room," Mary says, fanning her face with a program.

I roll my eyes. "He's accusing me of killing April. I'd say that calls for some heat."

Mary scoffs and waves a hand at me. "Everyone knows he's just trying to find a reason to talk to you. You've ignored him for fifteen years."

My mouth drops open. Is that why Travis is accusing me of murder? I doubt it. I was the last person to see April alive and I have motive. I'd suspect me too if I didn't know I was innocent.

"I have some information for you," Mary whispers, leaning in close to me. I can smell butterscotch on her breath.

"About what?"

Massage & Murder 39

"April."

I open my mouth to tell her to share it with the police, but pause. Maybe I do want to hear this. "What about her?"

"She was having an affair."

I gasp. "Are you sure?"

Mary nods. "With Dr. Gregory."

I gasp again. The guy's like twenty. Well maybe not that young, but he's young. Fresh out of med school. Came to Daysville a few months ago. "Does Bobby know?" I glance toward the front of the church where Bobby is gazing at his wife one last time before they close the casket.

Mary shakes her head. "I doubt it, but it's only a matter of time."

I frown and bite my lip. "Thank you for sharing this with me." I pause. "Why are you sharing this with me?"

"Because I know you. You're making a list of suspects. Trying to solve this case before the police. Prove your innocence. If anyone in this town can solve April's murder it's you." Mary pats my arm.

I quirk an eyebrow.

Mary laughs "You don't remember?"

I shake my head.

"In fourth grade, Margo May's cocker spaniel went missing. What was his name...Yawncy. Crazy name for an animal, but anyway, the police assumed it'd run off and brushed her off, but not you. You interrogated everyone. Followed the leads until you found that dog tied up in old Man West's abandoned barn where Ralph Taylor was keeping it because Margo stole his Pokemon cards. You got Ralph his cards back and Margo got her dog back.

I giggle then cough to cover it up since we're still technically at a funeral. The whole thing is coming back to me. I was really into Nancy Drew mysteries as a kid and was determined to solve that case. Maybe I really am an amateur sleuth.

Mary touches my arm and lowers her voice, "The police are not equipped for this. Murder doesn't happen here. You will solve this case, Autumn. Mark my words, you will. Just trust your instincts, follow your leads and your gut and for goodness sake be careful." She gives me a hug and hurries out the door.

I walk slowly toward the back of the church and across the parking lot to the town hall. My mind is racing with everything Mary just told me. Were the police incapable of solving this murder? Is that why Travis is so eager to pin this murder on me? Could I go to jail for a crime I didn't commit? The thought makes my stomach turn and growl all at the same time. It's lunch time and crime solving time. Bring on the food and suspects.

I yank open the door to the town hall and immediately am greeted with a blast of hot air. Paul, the gray-haired janitor takes my coat. Kind of fancy for a funeral. The smell of roast beef mixed with turkey and mashed potatoes wafts through the room. Three buffet tables are set up right inside the door and the line is to the door. I scan the sea of tables for Josh. He's at the far end stuffing his face. Go figure. A full plate is sitting across from him. I sigh with relief. The man's a saint.

"What took you so long?" Josh mumbles through a mouthful of food when I sit down across from him.

I roll my eyes and dig into my salad. "Manners. We're in public," I scold and glance around the table. Everyone is engrossed in their own conversations and doesn't notice my impolite BFF.

Josh swallows his food. "Again, what took you so long?"

"I had a couple of people to catch up with." I shrug and pick at my salad.

"You mean Travis."

I almost drop my fork. How did he know? Oh wait. Small town. Gossip. I'm surprised Travis and I aren't rumored to be back together by now. "I gave him and Cat my condolences."

Josh nods. His expression unreadable, which I know means he's mad. He has a great poker face, but when he plays it, it means he's masking his emotions and right now I know he's mad.

I change the subject. "Did you get a text from Vicky?"

"No. Why?" he mumbles.

I sigh. Thank goodness. "Travis told me the spa was able to re-open tomorrow. I thought maybe..."

"You thought maybe you were fired and I was holding out on you." Josh scoops up another forkful of roast beef, avoiding my eyes.

I blush. I can't help it. That's exactly what I thought, but didn't want Josh to think that. "I well... yes."

Josh shakes his head. I can tell he's disappointed in me. He finishes his plate, stands up and leaves. I watch him knowing he wouldn't actually leave me here. He gets in the dessert line. I sigh. I'm an idiot, but in my defense, it's been a tough week. Between finding a dead body on my table, being accused of murder by the love of my life, who I haven't talked to in fifteen years and dealing with all the rumors swirling around town, I'm bound to be a little paranoid.

Speaking of being paranoid, I can feel someone's eyes on me. The hairs on the back of my neck stand up. Sally. She's watching me from the buffet table. I get up and head in that direction, but she bolts. I mean flat out almost runs Mrs. Farmington from the grocery store over. No one else seems to notice, but Josh. He raises an eyebrow, shoves a brownie in his mouth and rushes to the coat closet. Good man.

I hurry toward the exit and push at the doors, but get some resistance.

"Umph," someone says from the other side of the door then I hear the scuffling of feet and a yelp.

Oh, no.

I crack open the door to find Travis splayed out on the ground. Cat is by his side trying to help him up. I cringe as Josh hands me my coat.

"What happened?" Josh peeks over my head. "Serves him right," he mumbles.

I elbow him, but he just smirks back at me.

Cat helps her dad to his feet while I open the door the rest of the way. "I'm so sorry."

Travis brushes the snow off his coat. "Where are you off to in such a hurry?"

I scan the parking lot in time to see a blue bug leaving the parking lot. Sally's car. Shoot. I missed her. At least I know where she lives.

"Autumn?"

Oh right, he asked me a question. "It's the weather. It's getting colder." The sun is shining down on us and the snow is starting to melt. A pile of snow drops from the roof with a plopping sound to emphasize my lie.

He grins, he knows I'm lying because I'm a terrible liar.

I hold my head high and squeeze past them. Josh places his hand on the small of my back and steers me toward the Jeep. I glance over my shoulder to find Travis staring at us. His eyes dark and broody. Jaw clenching. The man was angry and suspicious, but did he have to look like a model from GQ? Someone should lock him up for looking so hot. I flush, thankful we're outside so I can blame it on the cold air.

Josh unlocks the Jeep. I see a piece of paper flapping under the tire and bend down to pick it up. The squeal of tires sounds in the back of the parking lot, but I ignore it. The writing on the paper has me frozen. The next thing I know someone tackles me and I'm falling. "What the" I hit the ground hard. My knees burn, my side aches and something sharp scrapes my forehead. I taste snow and blood then everything goes black.

7
———

"Autumn. Autumn."

I groan. Why does it smell like bleach and vomit?

"Autumn. Wake-up."

I wish people would quit saying my name. It only makes my head hurt worse. My head. Why does my head hurt? I reach up and feel a bandage on it. My eyes are heavy as if someone is holding them shut. I'm able to open them just enough to see my best friend's face. I smile and try to sit up, but flinch. My ribs feel like someone made a punching bag out of them. In fact, every part of my body aches. Even my toes. "What happened?" I rasp. My throat feels like I ate a bunch of straw.

"Someone tried to run you over." Josh pats my hand.

It all comes back to me. I gasp and squeeze his hand. "You pushed me out of the way. You saved me."

Josh clenches his jaw and looks down at my hand.

"Actually, I saved you."

"Travis?" I turn toward his voice. He's hovering by the

window. His suit is covered in dark stains that appear to be a combination of grease and slush. "You saved me?"

He shrugs.

I bite my lip. "Thank you," I whisper holding his gaze for a moment. The world stops. My breathing hitches. The stupid heart machine gives me away and starts beeping rapidly. I hear Josh scoff next to me. Travis smiles and winks at me. There goes the beeping again. I take a deep breath and turn toward Josh. "Can we have a minute?"

Josh opens his mouth to say something then scoots back his chair and storms from the room.

I sigh and watch him go. This is the second time I've made him mad today. Is this day over yet?

Travis clears his throat.

I turn toward him. "What happened?"

"A dark SUV came speeding through the parking lot. You were busy reading a piece of paper you'd picked up and didn't see it coming."

"A dark SUV...did you see the plates?"

"Out of state."

"License number?"

He shook his head. "I was kind of busy making sure it didn't run us both over."

I nod. "A dark SUV with out of state plates was at the spa the same morning April was killed."

"Did you get the license plate number?"

I blush. "My eye sight isn't what it used to be."

He smirks.

"What?"

"Still trying to avoid getting glasses."

"I'm too young for glasses." I cross my arms and stick out my lower lip.

He laughs. "That's what you said in high school when you needed reading glasses."

"And I still think I'm too young for them."

"I think you would look cute in glasses."

I blush and glance away.

Travis clears his throat again and taps on his notepad. "I didn't get your statement the other day about the attempted break-in at the spa. Do you feel up to answering some questions?"

I nod.

"You showed up to work and found someone trying to pick the lock on the back door."

I nod again.

"Can you describe this person?"

"They were dressed in a black hoodie with a ski mask on their face. Medium height. Medium build."

"Anything else?"

I bite my lip then shake my head.

"Why would someone want to break into the spa?"

I shrug.

He sighs. "Autumn..." he pauses then holds up a piece of paper. "Can you explain this?"

I squint to read it then gasp. "I found that underneath the Jeep tire."

"So, you think it was meant for you?"

"Well someone tried to run me over so I'm pretty sure it was meant for me."

"*Stay out of this or you'll be next,*" Travis reads. "Stay out of what, Autumn?"

I bite my lip again.

"You're not investigating April's murder like you did that dumb dog in grade school, are you?"

Another shrug.

"Autumn, we're not talking about a dognapping. We're talking about murder. April was murdered."

"And you think I killed her," I shriek.

Travis shakes his head. "I have to look at all the facts. You had access to the kitchen knives, you have a motive and you were the last person to see her alive. I can't not suspect you..."

"So, I planted the note and hired someone to try and run me over with the hope you are watching and would push me out of the way."

His expression darkens.

"You really think I killed April, don't you?"

Travis opens his mouth, but then closes it.

"Get out." I point to the door.

"Autumn."

"GET OUT!" I scream. My head throbs from screaming. I grab it to keep it from exploding. My ribs ache for yelling and suddenly, I'm exhausted.

Josh comes running back in and gives me a once over. I'm also shaking and tears are streaking down my face. "You heard the lady, get out." A smug expression on his face.

Travis gives me a pleading look, but I simply glare at him. "I'm just doing my job, Autumn," he mumbles on the way out the door.

I want to tell him to 'do it better', but I refrain. He may be my cheating ex-boyfriend, but he's still a cop.

"Are you alright?" Josh rushes to my side and takes my hand.

I nod and wipe my eyes. "Someone tried to kill me." The emotions come full force and I'm sobbing and shaking. Josh climbs in next to me and holds me until I'm too exhausted to cry anymore. Then he tucks me in and I sleep. When I wake up, my head feels better and my body doesn't ache quite as much, they must have given me some pretty good pain killers. Josh is there reading a book. "I want to go home," I whisper.

He nods and sets down his book. "The doctor is making his rounds now. We'll ask."

I smile and close my eyes. The threatening note plays in my mind. "Who do you think killed April?"

Josh clears his throat and I open my eyes as he shakes his head. "You're investigating this, aren't you?"

"How can I not? Travis is trying to pin this murder on me. Mary told me the police aren't equipped to solve this murder. They're looking for a scape goat and I don't plan to be one."

"Autumn, as much as I would like to believe Travis isn't capable of solving this murder, the guy knows what he's doing."

I snort.

"You know he does."

I pursue my lips and roll my eyes.

"He found the teenagers that were breaking all those windows?"

I scoff. "We're not talking about solving a minor criminal action, we're talking about murder. There has never been a murder in this town. Jaywalking and speeding are the biggest crimes committed around here. Travis is in over his head and he knows it. The captain is going to retire soon and I bet Travis is gunning for his job. If he finds April's murderer then it will put him in the running. I'm an easy fall girl."

"Autumn, you're being silly. He won't put you in jail unless you're guilty."

I glare at him. I hate when he makes sense, but I still don't think Travis can solve this murder, not to mention it looks like the killer is after me now. I need to solve this case and fast.

Josh sighs. "I think Nikki has just as much motive as you do to kill April and she was at the spa."

I smile at him. There's my best friend and side kick. "Not to mention Vicky."

He frowns. "Vicky?"

"April was talking about opening another spa. It's motive."

"I don't think Vicky would kill April over that."

"The spa means everything to her."

"Sure, but murder? That seems extreme...crazy." Josh runs a hand through his hair as his phone beeps. He slips it from his pocket. "Speaking of Vicky. She says the spa is re-opening tomorrow and wants to know if we're ready to get back to work. What should I tell her?" He glances at my bandaged head.

"I'm fine." I sit up in the bed and keep a smile plastered to my face even when every muscle in my body protests. "We need to get back to the scene of the crime."

Josh groans. "The police have gathered all the evidence. There won't be anything there for us to find."

I smirk. "You're probably right, but it doesn't hurt to check again."

He sends a text back to Vicky as he shakes his head. "You were almost run over by a beast of a vehicle and now you want to traipse around town looking for clues to try to catch a killer."

"With the help of my strong and protective best friend." I bat my eyelashes.

Josh grins and laughs before flexing an arm. "I am pretty strong."

"Incredibly." I giggle. "No one will mess with me when I have you with me."

His eyes grow dark and his expression turns serious. "Promise me you won't do anything stupid. Don't go anywhere dangerous alone."

"Dangerous? In Daysville? There's not a dangerous spot in town."

"Autumn," he growls.

"Fine. I promise." I hold up my right hand as if I'm on the witness stand, except my other hand has my fingers crossed underneath the blanket. I love Josh. He's my sidekick, but he doesn't have the guts to do what needs to be done. I know having him in my corner is essential to figuring out this case without him telling Travis. Plus having someone to bounce scenarios and suspects off of will be nice. "Now, who else should we add to the suspect list?"

Josh shrugs and lowers his voice. "Everyone hated April, but enough to kill her, I'm not sure."

"What about Sally?"

"Sally? Why would she kill April?"

"April insulted her massage the day she was murdered. Refused to have Sally work on her."

Josh nods. "Makes sense. April liked deep tissue massage. Sally definitely doesn't have that skill."

"Why do you think Sally became a massage therapist?"

He frowns. "What do you mean?"

"I mean she doesn't love it. Not like we do."

Josh smirks. "No one loves massage like we do. We're massage nerds. No other therapists quiz each other on the different muscles and attachment points."

I laugh. "I'm not saying she has to, but she always seems so bored. Like she'd rather be anywhere else and when she does get a client, she almost seems scared."

"Scared?"

"Yeah like she's afraid to work on them."

"Well she doesn't have a lot of experience. Vicky told me she just graduated about a month ago before she moved to town. It's probably just nerves."

I bite my lip. "Maybe, but it seems like something more."

Josh rolls his eyes. "You're reading into things, Autumn."

I open my mouth to protest when Dr. Gregory walks in.

8

Dr. Gregory smiles, but it doesn't reach his eyes, which are red rimmed and glassy. His black hair is slicked back. He reminds me of a young Keanu Reeves in a lab coat.

"How are you feeling Miss Fisher?"

I cringe. I hate being called Miss Fisher. Reminds me of my school days when I was talking too much in class and my teachers would call me out on it. "Better. Can I go home?"

He makes a note on his iPad. "Let me do a couple of tests then we'll talk." He eyes Josh. "Are you the boyfriend?"

I groan. Does everyone think we're secretly dating?

Josh grins. "Just the best friend. I'm going to grab you some tea." He pats my hand and slips out the door.

"Best friend?" Dr. Gregory raises an eyebrow.

I shrug. "I'm a lucky girl."

He pulls a light pen from his pocket and shines it in my eyes. "I'll say." He clicks off the pen. "You're lucky that SUV didn't make you a pancake."

I frown and raise an eyebrow, unsure of his strange bedside manner.

"Sorry. I'm not myself today."

"Because of April?"

Now it's his turn to frown. "What do you mean?" Then unwraps my bandage and checks it. "It's just a scratch. Probably cut it on rocks." Then he re-wraps it.

"I know you two were having an affair."

He shakes his head and looks out the window. "How did you find out?"

"It's a small town."

"Too small. Sometimes I wonder why I moved here."

"Why did you move here?"

"Because of April. I had a new fertility treatment she was trying. Everyone in town knew she wanted another baby...with Bobby." He gets up and walks to the window.

"Does Bobby know about the affair?"

He turns to me with a serious expression on his face. "Do you think I would be alive right now if he did?"

The man has a point. I couldn't see Bobby taking that news very well. Although he wouldn't go after April, he would go after the doctor. But would someone who loves Bobby go after April if they found out about the affair? My thoughts float to Nikki.

"April was upset about the affair. Quit her treatments. Decided she and Bobby were happy without a child."

"And were you?"

"Was I what?"

"Upset about ending the affair?"

"It was a mistake. We both realized it. I just got out of a serious relationship and wasn't looking for anything especially with a patien-" his words are cut off by yelling at the nurse's station.

"Bobby," I whisper and lock eyes with the doctor.

He goes pale and looks about ready to faint. "He's going to kill me."

I want to tell him that he won't, but then I see Bobby tearing down the hallway and I can't be sure. Someone cuts him off. Travis. Bobby pushes him out of the way like he's tossing a ragdoll then practically takes the door off the hinges flinging it open.

"You!" Bobby points a finger at Dr. Gregory.

"It was a mistake." Dr. Gregory holds up his hands to protect to his face.

Bobby balls his fists, his nostrils are flaring and his jaw is clenching and unclenching. "You slept with my wife," he growls

"I'm sorry."

Bobby's eyes narrow and he lunges for Dr. Gregory as Travis and Josh tackle him to the ground. "Let me go! He slept with my WIFE!"

"Get out of here NOW!" Travis yells at Dr. Gregory, who doesn't have to be told twice.

I open my mouth to inquire about going home, but decide now isn't the time. I can only hope he signs my discharge papers.

Josh slams the door shut with his foot and works with Travis to get Bobby to sit down in a chair. Travis has Bobby's arms pinned behind his back and is clicking on a pair of handcuffs.

"You can't arrest me. I haven't done anything." Bobby struggles against the cuffs.

Travis opens his mouth, but I interrupt him. "Bobby, who told you about the affair?"

Bobby blinks and focuses on me like he didn't realize I was here. "A note. Slipped underneath our front door. I found it when I got home from the cemetery."

"A note? Do you still have it?"

He shakes his head. "I left it on the kitchen table."

I bite my lip not sure I should pry especially since he's a grieving husband, but I need to eliminate Bobby as a suspect and Travis doesn't seem to be upset I'm asking questions. He's still trying to catch his breath so I continue, "Did you suspect April of having an affair?"

"No. Never. April and I were still trying to have a baby. We were happy except..."

"Except what?"

"Well the past few weeks she'd been acting weird. Starting new business. Crying one minute then happy the next. I figured it was from the hormone shots, but then all the sudden she says she stopped treatments and we need to work on our marriage. Decides Cat needs to go to boarding school. That it will help her get into a better college. I knew something was up, but I didn't pry."

Travis clenches his jaw. "She makes straight A's, she's going to get into a good college."

Bobby scoffs. "I know that, but she's April's daughter. It was her decision."

"Not just her decision."

"Well it's not anymore, now is it?" Bobby snaps.

The men glare at each other for a moment then a nurse pops her head in the door. "Detective, there's a call for you at the nurse's station. They said it was urgent."

"Don't move," Travis orders Bobby then glances at Josh and nods.

Josh rolls his eyes, but places a hand on Bobby's shoulder.

Travis casts me a sideways glance before heading out the door.

Once he's out of earshot, I know it's my chance to get

some more answers. "Bobby, do you know who killed April?"

He sighs and hangs his head. "No one liked her. It wasn't a secret." He sighs again and looks up at me. "I shouldn't be telling you this, but a couple of weeks ago I came home early from a business meeting and found her and the Mayor arguing in the living room."

"What were they arguing about?"

Another sigh. "The Mayor's broke."

"Broke? What do you mean?"

"I mean he's got nothing. He's deep in debt. Spent every last cent of his fortune...of April's inheritance."

I gasp.

"April was livid. I figured that's why she stopped fertility treatments although we have plenty of money. It's not like she needed her inheritance, but the treatments weren't cheap and it's not like they were working. I guess I wasn't meant to be a dad." Bobby looks down at the floor.

I feel tears brimming and quickly blink them away, but not before Josh sees and cocks his head at me. I shake my head and clear my throat, tapping down my own desire to one day have kids although it's looking bleak. "Do you think the Mayor killed April?"

Bobby's head snaps back up. "No." Then he pauses. "I mean I don't know. He has a life insurance policy on April. Has since she was a little girl...but kill his own daughter for money. We were helping him...paying his debts off, but last week April told me to quit paying his bills. Said she found something that made her question her father."

"Did she say what she found?"

Bobby shakes his head. "She told me she was looking into it and would tell me when she found proof."

"So, did you stop paying his bills?"

Bobby nods then his eyes get wide. "The Mayor threatened April last Saturday...two days before she was killed. Told her she'd be sorry for interfering."

"Interfering in what?

Bobby shrugs. "No clue."

"Have you told any of this to the police?" I see Travis coming down the hall.

"Not until I find out what the Mayor is hiding."

"So why tell me?"

Bobby smiles. "Margo May."

I smile back. Solving that dognapping case is sure coming in handy.

Travis walks in and motions for Bobby to stand up. "I'll walk you out. Dr. Gregory is in the process of filing a restraining order against you so I don't want to see or hear that you're anywhere near this hospital or his home, understood?"

Bobby nods then as Travis steps behind him to unlock his cuffs, he mouths. "*I'll call you.*"

I smirk as I watch the men leave. Travis peeks back at me. His expression unreadable. I look away not wanting to deal with him or the butterflies dancing in my belly every time I see him. I turn toward Josh. "The Mayor just got added to our suspect list. I need to get out of here."

9
―――――

"I need all hands-on deck. Sally called in sick and the spa is booked solid today. Everyone is requesting you, Autumn," Vicky says, staring at the computer screen.

"Me?" I raise an eyebrow at Josh.

Vicky nods. "Seems everyone wants to talk to the new sleuth in town. Determine if they're on your suspect list."

I gulp. "My suspect list? That's ridiculous. I don't have a suspect list."

"You don't?" Vicky straightens and narrows her eyes at me.

I shake my head and try to look innocent. The bell above the door rings and a blast of cold air blows in the waiting room.

"Oh, Autumn. Just the person I was wanting to see." Nikki stomps her feet on the mat. "Can I talk to you for a moment?"

I open my mouth to respond when Vicky cuts in, "Autumn has a full schedule today. Her first client is waiting. You'll have to talk to her when she's not working." Vicky hands me a file and pushes me toward the green room. I check the time and see I'm five minutes late. I groan, this will make me late all day. I wash my hands and briefly glance at the file folder. It's a new client.

Michael Millum.

Hmm. Must be someone traveling through or someone new has moved to town and I'm not up on the town gossip.

Knocking softly, I enter the room, the table is empty. I step in and the door shuts behind me. My palms begin to sweat and I feel like I've just walked into a trap. Could April's killer be behind me? I gulp and turn slowly. "Travis! What are you doing in here? You scared me to death." I smack him in the gut. He doesn't even flinch. Stupid six-pack.

"Sorry. I didn't mean to scare you. I wanted to talk to you. Figured this was the only way."

"The only way? Have you not heard of a phone? You know where I live."

He runs a hand through his red hair. "I don't have your number and I went by your house...you weren't alone."

"So, you make up a fake name and stalk me at my work?" I gesture to the file.

Travis smirks. "It's not a fake name. I use it as my alias when I'm undercover."

I cross my arms over my chest. "Alias? Since when does police work in Daysville require undercover work?"

His eyes grow dark. "I don't just work in Daysville."

"You don't?"

He shakes his head.

I narrow my eyes. "Where else do you work?"

"In Kansas City and St. Louis. I help out on a few cases every now and then to make some extra money."

I nod. "What kind of cases?"

"If I told you well you know…"

I roll my eyes then frown. "Are you in danger?"

He shrugs. "It comes with being a cop."

"Not in Daysville."

He shrugs again. "I need the money. Daysville cops don't make much. I have a kid. Bills." He pauses. "I'm up for Captain, if I get it then I'll quit my side gigs.

"I see." I cross my arms and try not to let him see how much the thought of him being in danger affects me. "So, you want to talk. Talk. I'm surprised you don't just drag me down to the station? Interrogate me since you think I'm guilty."

Travis sighs. "I'm just doing my job, Autumn. You have a motive. You also have means and opportunity."

I snort. "So, do you."

His eyes grow dark and his jaw tightens. "What do you mean?"

"Cat. April was planning to send her away to boarding school. You two were going to court over it. You were in the break room the day she was murdered, right by the knives. You too have means, motive and opportunity."

Travis scowls. "The rumor mill is really churning. We weren't going to court. How did you know I was here?"

"It's a small town, Travis. Bethany told me a cop was here to question me about the attempted break-in. You were the first officer on the scene. Only…" I bite my lip, thinking back to that awful day. "You came in through the front door, but Bethany told me you were waiting in the break room."

"I can see your mind putting the puzzle together. You are investing this case, aren't you?" He rubs his eyes then winces.

"What's wrong?"

He rubs his shoulder. "Nothing."

"Nothing my eye. What's hurting?"

"Really, Autumn. I'm fine." He moves his shoulder to prove it, but ends up flinching.

"Lie down."

"Excuse me?"

"Take off your shirt and lie down on the table."

"No. I'm here to talk not get a massage."

"Vicky is charging you either way so you might as well let me work on your back."

He scoffs. "Fine."

I smirk. "You're the only person I know that complains about getting a massage."

He starts to unbutton his shirt and I turn my back to him. "Slip under the sheet and lie face down with your head in the face rest." The massage table creaks and I hear shuffling. When the room goes quiet, I turn around and oil my hands. "Where does it hurt?"

"Here." He taps his trapezius muscle. "It's been killing me for weeks."

"And you're just now getting a massage?"

"I've been kind of busy."

I snort.

"What? I have."

"Busy with what?"

"Work."

"Work? What kind of work? Daysville hasn't had anything exciting happen since well last summer. The high school kids breaking windows." I run an elbow down his back.

He moans. "Oh man. That feels good. You really did find your calling."

I smile. I can't help it. His words warm my heart and then he changes the subject and says something stupid.

"Have you ever thought of killing April?"

"I believe we were discussing your motive, detective." I put an elbow into his shoulder blade and he groans.

"I didn't kill April. Sure, I was mad, she was trying to send Cat away, but we would have worked it out. April had been acting strange the past few weeks. Making erratic demands...more than her usual ones.

"What do you mean by 'erratic demands'?"

He moans again when I knead the muscle back and forth. His voice comes out sleepy and he yawns before saying, "I shouldn't be telling you this, but the whole thing is ridiculous. She wanted me to investigate City Hall. Look into the Mayor's spending habits."

"Did she say why?"

"She thought he was doing something illegal."

"Like what?"

"She didn't know. Hence the investigation."

"Did you look into it?"

Austin shakes his head. "I can't just open an investigation into City Hall without proof. It's career suicide."

"I bet April didn't like that." I move to work on his neck.

"That's when she started threatening to send Cat to boarding school. Told me if I didn't look into City Hall and the Mayor, she would send her away."

I gasp. "So, she was blackmailing you?"

"Not really blackmailing."

"What do you call threatening someone to get them to do what you want?"

Travis doesn't respond.

I continue to work on his back in silence. Thinking about everything he just told me.

His deep voice interrupts my thoughts. "Why didn't you let me explain about April in high school?"

The question catches me off guard. "I-I You broke my heart, Travis." Emotion catches in my throat and I choke it down. Tears come quickly and I can't blink them back. One falls on his leg.

He stiffens. "I-I saw you."

"Saw me what?" I cover his back and move to the front of the table.

"You and Josh." He lifts his head and stares at me.

"Me and Josh?"

Travis opens to his mouth to answer when a muffled scream comes from another room. He jumps up, thank the Lord he left his pants on, shrugs on his shirt and hurries from the room. I follow him, trying to get the vision of his bare chest out of my mind.

"What the-" Travis stops outside the break room door.

I peek over his shoulder to find Bethany helping her mother up from the floor. Ceramic is scattered on the floor and blood is dripping from a gash on Vicky's forehead. "Stay put," I gesture to Travis's bare feet. "We don't need two people bleeding." I rush forward and snag a towel. "What happened?"

"Someone was trying to break-in again." Vicky blinks.

"She's in shock." Bethany pats her hand and helps her to the couch. "She might have a concussion."

I pat the towel on her wound and check the cut. "Did you see who tried to break in?"

"N-No. Someone in black. I was getting some tea and heard scraping at the back door. When I opened it, I must have surprised them as they did me. My feet got caught up on the rug and I lost my balance, hit my head on the counter and broke my favorite mug."

"I need to get her to the hospital." Bethany gets up and moves toward the coat rack.

"I'll take you." Travis rushes from the room and is back within seconds with his coat and shoes on.

"What about the front desk? Who'll answer the phones. Bethany, you have to stay. Detective Mills can take me." Vicky pats her daughter's hand.

"But..." Bethany bites her lip as if she's torn on what to do. She looks at me.

I want to offer to watch the front desk and answer phones, but my schedule is full. We can't leave the desk unattended especially if someone is trying to break-in to steal something. Might as well put a sign out front, which says, Come and take what you want.

"I can watch the front desk," Nikki says from the doorway. "My classes don't start until five and the spa closes at four so I'm happy to help. You go with your mother, Bethany."

"Really? Are you sure?" Bethany's eyes fill with tears.

Nikki nods. "Definitely. Your mother needs you."

Bethany jumps up and hugs Nikki. "Thank you so much. I'll be back before we close and if I can't, I'll text you."

"Josh and I can close up. Take your mother home and get some rest. It's been a long week."

"Oh, thank you, Autumn!" Bethany pulls me in for a hug before snagging their coats.

Travis helps Vicky into her coat and ushers her toward the door. "We're not done with our talk. Will you be home later?"

"No."

"No?" He quirks an eyebrow.

"I have a class tonight."

"A class?"

"Yes."

"What kind of class?"

"I hate to interrupt, but we really need to get mom to the hospital. She looks about ready to pass out."

"Right. Let's go." Travis shoots me a suspicious look before leaving then calls over his shoulder. "I'll send an officer to dust the back door for prints." Then he was gone.

10

"Why didn't you tell him you were attending my yoga class?" Nikki asks from behind me.

I jump almost forgetting she was there. "I don't know. I guess I'm just having a hard time seeing him. Being around him."

She looks down at the ground. "I know what you mean. Seeing Bobby always throws me for a loop too."

"Speaking of Bobby. Have you talked to him lately?"

Nikki bites her lip. "We had lunch last week. Well not really lunch. I was picking up some supplies for the studio in Villsboro and stopped in the little diner there and Bobby was there eating too. He offered for me to join him. It was awkward at first, but then we fell into easy conversation and it was like no time has passed." She sighs.

"So, you still love Bobby?"

She blushes. "You still love Travis. They're our soulmates."

I shake my head. "I'm not in love with Travis and he's not my soulmate."

Nikki rolls her eyes and smirks. "Denial doesn't look good on you." The phone rings and she heads toward the receptionist desk.

I follow. "We're not in high school anymore, Nikki. Travis cheated on me. Had a kid...with my ex best friend. Some things are unforgivable."

She gives me another doubtful look and picks up the phone. Makes a note on the schedule and hangs up then turns to me. "Autumn, Travis has done his time. Served his sentence. Spent the last fifteen years trying to get over you. April is dead. It's time to move on. Forgive him and start fresh."

I frown. "You make it sound so simple. Is that what you plan to do with Bobby?"

She shrugs. "We had a nice talk last week."

"Before April ended up dead."

Nikki turns red. "Well...yes, it was a week before she died."

"Did Bobby give you a reason to think he wanted to get back together with you?"

"Well...no. I mean he said he was in love with April. Was committed to their marriage."

"And now that she's dead, you think he'll commit to you?"

Nikki bites her lip.

I narrow my eyes and study her. "You and April had a fight at the garden club the night before she died. What was that about?"

Nikki studies her nails.

"Nikki. What did you and April fight about?"

"Bobby," she whispers.

"What about Bobby?" I lean against the desk.

"She found out we had lunch. Went crazy."

"How did she find out?"

"Bobby told her. Guess they told each other everything." She rolls her eyes.

"Did she have a reason to go 'crazy'?"

"What?! No! You know April…knew April. She blew it up into this big thing. Accused me of having an affair with her husband, which is ridiculous and why should she care, she was sleeping with Dr. Gregory."

I gasp. "How did you find out?"

"Oh, everyone knows." Nikki waves a hand as though it's no big deal. "Bobby even knows. I told him."

"You told Bobby last week that April was having an affair."

"Well, not last week. I slipped a note underneath his door yesterday."

I gape at her. "Are you crazy? The man almost ripped Dr. Gregory limb from limb. Now, Dr. Gregory has a restraining order against him."

Nikki's eyes grow big.

"Why would you do that?"

She hangs her head. "Seeing him in so much pain is killing me. I thought if he knew April was cheating on him, he could get over her easier."

"So, he could move on, with you."

"Eventually. Thought we could start as friends then maybe…become more."

I shake my head. "Nikki, who told you April was having an affair?"

"I saw her and Dr. Gregory together. Mary and I were having a meeting about the fundraiser for the children's wing and we saw them kissing outside his office."

"When was this?"

"About a month ago."

"Did you confront April about the affair?"

"During our fight at the garden club. Well in the parking lot after everyone went home. I waited for her by her car. She was all jumpy. Acting really weird. She broke down about the affair. Tried to bribe me not to tell Bobby."

"Bribe you with what?"

Nikki gives me a look. "What do you think? Money, of course."

"Do you need money?"

Nikki blushes. "The studio does well, but I've been saving up to do some more training. She promised me the money if I kept my mouth shut. I'm glad I didn't tell Bobby about the affair at our lunch. I was so wrapped up in how good it was to talk to him, it completely slipped my mind." She sighs. "Of course, I didn't get the money because she was killed the next day."

"So, you didn't really have a reason to kill April?"

She makes a face. "No. I mean I won't deny I haven't thought about killing her over the years. I'm sure you have too, but to actually kill someone." Nikki pauses and shakes her head. "That's not very Namaste if you know what I mean." She puts her hands together and bows to me.

I quirk an eyebrow. "I thought Namaste meant hello or thank you."

"It does, but in some cultures, it also means 'giving peace and forgiveness'. I forgave April a long time ago for stealing Bobby although I'm not sure she actually did."

"What do you mean?"

"Can anyone really be stolen? I mean Bobby wasn't hypnotized. He chose to be with April. Faults and all. He wasn't even drunk like Travis."

"Drunk? Travis was drunk?" I frown and try to process that fact. "He didn't drink. Ever."

"Well, he did that night. I was at the party and he showed up drunk and kept right on drinking until April began flirting with him. Then those two disappeared and well nine months later, Cat appeared."

I frown and bite my lip. "Why was he drinking? Was he upset?"

Nikki shrugs. "He was mumbling about you and Josh."

"Me and Josh? That's what he said earlier. He saw me and Josh."

"He saw you what?" Nikki props her hands on her chin. "Did you and Josh get together in high school?"

I give her a look and crinkle my nose. "What? No."

"Ahh."

"What's with the 'ahh'? Why does everyone think we are or should be a couple?"

"Because you two are inseparable. You're also adorable together. You and Travis were cute together, but I've always been rooting for Josh. He followed...follows you around like a love-sick puppy. You really need to throw him a bone." She wiggles her eyebrows at me.

I smack her arm. "Back to you. Why do you think Bobby chose April over you? I mean you two are so different."

"Because she blackmailed me," Bobby said, walking in behind Josh. "Thanks for working on my foot, man." He slips Josh a twenty then hands him his credit card for payment.

I glance at Nikki. Her mouth is hanging open in shock. I don't blame her. I'm kind of shocked too. "What do you mean she blackmailed you?" April really was the worst. Seducing Travis while he was drunk, blackmailing Bobby. What was wrong with her? "But you married her. Stayed married to her. Said you two were happy."

"We were...eventually." He pauses then sighs and leans

against the counter. "April's gone. The truth needs to come out. I've kept this secret for over fifteen years. About time I come clean."

"We won't tell anyone." Nikki reaches over the counter and squeezes his hand.

He places his other one over hers and they stare at each other for a moment. "I'd appreciate it if this stays between us. I was planning to tell you at lunch last week, but couldn't find the nerve. I never wanted you to blame yourself for what happened between us. I mean we were happy. In love. That's what April couldn't stand. She hated happiness. Hated Love. Well unless it was her happiness. Her love. She had something on me I couldn't tell her no, it would have ended me. My reputation. My dreams and yours. I couldn't let her destroy us. Even if it meant there was no longer an us."

Nikki blinks back tears and I do too.

Josh clears his throat and holds up Bobby's credit card. Typical man ruining a sweet moment with stuff like credit cards.

She blushes then moves to the side so he can run it.

"Where's Bethany?" Josh asks, swiping Bobby's card.

Nikki opens her mouth, but I cut her off. "Long story. I'll tell you later. Nikki is filling in and we're closing up. Now, back to blackmail. How was April blackmailing you?"

He gulps. "I was cheating."

Nikki and I gasp. She pulls back her hand as if his touch burned her.

He scrunches up his face and rakes a hand through his hair. "Not like that. Not on you." We must not look convinced because he sighs and continues, "I was paying a kid in Villsboro to do my homework, my papers, even slip me the answers to tests." We gasp and he scowls, "Football was consuming me. Coach was expecting me to be bigger, faster, even my dad was riding me. I couldn't keep up with the pressure and with school. Something had to give."

"So, you cheated," Nikki whispers as if trying to wrap her head around the bomb he just dropped.

Bobby nods. "April found out. Threatened to tell the coach. I would have been kicked off the team, would've lost my scholarship to Mizzou. It would have killed my momma...embarrassed you." He holds out a hand to Nikki. She hesitates then accepts it. "I'm sorry. I should have told you." He hangs his head. "I was so ashamed. Embarrassed. I didn't want to embarrass my family or you." He looks up and locks eyes with Nikki. "I didn't want to end up working in my dad's hardware store."

"Your dad made a good living," Nikki squeezes his hand.

"I know, but it was never the life I wanted. You knew that. I was going to play in the NFL before I blew my knee out my junior year of college."

I study him as he and Nikki seem lost in their own work then ask, "So, what were the terms of this blackmail? Dating? Marriage? Live a life with her so she doesn't expose your secret?"

He turns to me and says, "At first she just made me break up with Nikki. Date her."

"Then she found out she was pregnant," I mutter, the memory still painful.

Bobby rubs the back of his neck. "Funny thing about that. I don't remember actually sleeping with April in high school. One night is a little fuzzy. I got kind of drunk. Missing you," he squeezes Nikki's hand.

She blushes.

"April claimed that was the night we conceived Cat."

"But you didn't. She was already pregnant."

Bobby nods. "My mother told me to marry her so I did. Would have raised Cat as mine too, but when she came out with all that red hair, I knew she wasn't mine. No one in our family has red hair and everyone knew April had slept with Travis. It was a no brainer."

"So why stay married to her?"

"She still threatened to tell the coach I was cheating if I divorced her. She was worried about her image, which I'm pretty sure was ruined when she slept with Travis then married me, but I wasn't in a position to tell her that. I went off to Mizzou. Figured she'd get bored of being home with a baby and divorce me, but she didn't. When I graduated, I came back here and the Mayor set me up with a job. We just fell into a routine. Became a family. It worked."

My head's throbbing. This is all so bizarre. April was more manipulative than I thought. Who else did she blackmail enough for them to want her dead?

The bell rings above the door, we all jump, "Am I late?" Mrs. Ryder, my weekly eleven a.m. client asks, pulling her wool hat off her head and shaking out her gray curls.

"Right on time," I say and lead her back to the lavender room. "Take your time and I'll be right back." I close the door and hurry back toward the front. Josh is leading Miss Viles toward the blue room. "Wait, use the green room." I gesture down the hall. Josh gives me a strange look, but does as I ask.

I have to look in there before someone uses the room. Although I have no idea what I'm looking for or hoping to find. Taking a deep breath, I peek in the blue room. The room is lit and ready for a client. No blood. No dead body on the table. No one would ever know April was killed in here except they do, it was in the paper.

The room has a creepy vibe. Even the lavender essential

oil being diffused in the room isn't soothing my nerves. I walk around the table and step on something. It's a blue hair tie. I squat down and study it. I wear black hair ties and this is clearly blue. My ponytail was also very intact when I last left this room. I think about my suspect list. Vicky doesn't wear hair ties. Her hair is too short. Nikki wears them, but after talking with her, I'm thinking about taking her off the list. Travis, Bobby and the Mayor don't wear hair ties. That leaves Sally. I think back to the day of the murder. Sally was MIA. Although I didn't really look for her, I don't remember seeing her anywhere. Bethany and Vicky were holed up in Vicky's office calling clients and cancelling appointments all while cooperating with the investigation, but Sally wasn't anywhere to be found. Where had she disappeared to and why?

"Autumn?"

I jump and almost fall forward into the massage table, but reach out in time to catch myself. "You scared me." I glare at my BFF.

Josh smirks and leans against the door frame, crossing his arms. "I thought I'd find you in here."

I roll my eyes at him. "It's a good thing I came in here. I think I found something." I grab a tissue and pick up the hair tie.

He pushes off the door frame and moves toward me. "What is it?"

I hold it up.

He raises an eyebrow. "It's a hair tie."

"I know."

"So. Any woman could have dropped it."

I shake my head. "I vacuumed this rug on Saturday before I left. There was no hair tie. My hair was in a ponytail. April wouldn't be caught dead with a hair tie." I cringe at the words. "You know what I mean. Her hair was short. She had no reason to wear a hair tie."

"Maybe it's Bethany's? She does turn on the lights and heat packs when she comes in."

"Or it's Sally's?"

Josh's eyes grow wide.

"I think we need to take 'sick' Sally some soup."

11

"What a day?" I yawn and turn off the light in the break room.

"You're telling me. I smell like a women's perfume counter." Josh sniffs his scrub top and makes a face. "Every woman in town gave me hug. Something about April's death in my workplace causing me trauma. I don't feel traumatized except maybe now I do with all those chemical induced hugs. Is there such as thing as Perfume Trauma?"

I stifle a grin. "Don't act like you hated it. Especially when the music teacher, Miss Violet Viles gave you one. I saw your face. You were enjoying it." I poke his ribs.

He turns red. "She's kind of cute."

"You should ask her out."

"She's a client."

"Usually my client."

"You were booked. I was her only option."

"So."

"So, she's still a client."

"She doesn't have to be. I can work on her from here on out or Sally can if I'm booked."

"Speaking of Sally, are you planning to talk to her?"

"Nice try changing the subject."

He shrugs. "Are you?"

I nod. "I sent her a text asking if she was feeling up to visitors. She thought she might still be 'contagious', but wanted to know if we could meet her for breakfast. Thought it was just a twenty-four-hour bug." I roll my eyes because I'm not buying the sick act. "Now, back to you. Are you going to ask out Violet or not?"

"I don't know. Do you really think I should?"

I slip into my coat and grab my yoga mat. "Sure, why not?"

"It's just...well. Never mind." He shrugs on his coat. "Wanna come over for dinner and a movie after your yoga class?"

"You could ask Violet to join you for dinner and a movie. I'm sure she would love it."

His face turns red again and he looks uncomfortable.

I chuckle and change the subject before he clams up like he does when he wants to avoid discussing something, "You could join me for yoga then we could grab Sushi, maybe go dancing."

Josh makes a face like I just asked him if he wanted to hang out with a pack of hungry wolves.

I burst out laughing. "Okay. Scratch that. No yoga, sushi or dancing for you."

He hesitates. "Maybe I should go with you."

"Why?" I open the back door and come face to face with the person dressed in black. Their brown eyes look familiar. They take off running and Josh takes off after them.

Car tires squeal in the distance. The same dark SUV

with out of town plates. I hear a siren in the distance although I'm not sure how they knew someone was trying to break-in again. Maybe the police will finally catch this guy... or girl. From their build, I'm guessing it's a guy.

Josh comes back to me huffing and puffing then bends over placing his hands on his knees. "I really need to hit the treadmill more."

I pat his back and laugh. "Did you happen to catch the license plate number?"

He shakes his head. "I was too busy trying to catch them and not break my neck. The parking lot is solid ice. I kept falling. They must have spikes on their shoes because they didn't fall once." He huffs, smoke coming out his mouth. "I'm going to call the police."

Sirens and lights come barreling into the parking lot, sliding to a stop in front of Regina's salon. Travis jumps out and hurries inside. A fire truck and a couple firemen get out right behind him.

Josh and I exchange a look, lock the door and head to the Salon. Hair chemicals mixed with smoke are the first things I smell. Smoke lingers in the waiting area. Travis is trying to calm Regina down. She's crying and mascara is running down her cheeks. I cough and wave smoke away from my face. "Leave the door open."

Josh opens the door wider even though it's freezing, the salon is like an inferno.

"What happened?" I head over to Regina and Travis.

Regina has her face in Travis's chest, clinging onto his suit coat, her wailing is muffled. He's patting her on the back. He mouths "Fire".

Well, duh. Any idiot could figure that out. Seeing he wasn't going to give me any more details, I move toward the back of the Salon. Ted, an older fireman is hosing down a charred part of the back wall of the Salon. The window is broken and a flashlight is rolling around on the floor.

"Hey, Autumn. Is the spa alright?"

"I think so. Why?"

"Someone threw a flashlight through the window. It knocked over a candle and well." He gestures to the wall. "It could have been a lot worse. Luckily, Regina was here cleaning up or this place would have been gone in seconds. All these flammable products." He shakes his head.

"A flashlight? What a weird thing to throw through a window. Why not a rock?"

Ted shrugs. "All the rocks are covered in ice, may have been the only thing they had."

I bend down to look at the flashlight. There's nothing special about it. Black with a silver ring around the top.

"Don't touch it," Travis orders from behind me. He snaps a picture then outlines it with spray paint.

"Aren't you going to bag it for prints."

He shoots me a look. "It's too hot right now. I'll have to wait till it cools."

"Right." I blush and glance around, taking in the damage.

"Josh said the intruder was trying to break into the spa again. I wonder if we're dealing with the same person."

"Maybe. Use the fire as a distraction." I rush to the front of the salon and toward the spa.

"Autumn, what are you doing?" Josh calls after me.

"I think the fire is a distraction. We need to check the spa." I turn the corner and see the back door to the spa wide open.

"Hold up, Autumn," Travis says, pushing me to the side and taking out his gun. "They could still be in there."

The sound of file cabinets opening and closing is coming from inside.

Travis puts a finger to his lips. "Stay here," He whispers then disappears inside.

I glance at Josh and motion for him to follow me.

He grabs my arm and shakes his head. I shake him off and head inside, knowing he'll follow me. I tiptoe into the break room, careful not to squeak my shoes on the tile floor. Josh's sneakers squeak behind me and I freeze. The shuffling stops in the reception area then footsteps pound toward us.

Travis steps out from the shadows and grabs the person. They fight against him, even take a few swings at him before connecting with his nose. He staggers back and lets go. Josh moves to intercept them, but his shoes are wet and he slips on the tile. I stick out my foot to trip them and they skid across the floor, but scramble up before we can reach them. Josh and Travis take off after him, slipping on the icy parking lot.

I flip on the light and make my way to the front of the spa. The file cabinet drawers are open. Scrapes on the lock show it'd been picked since we lock it every night. A few client files are sticking out, which doesn't make any sense. Why would this person be looking at client files?

"Don't touch anything, Autumn."

I jump. "Did you catch him?"

Travis shakes his head, wipes his nose with the back of his hand where blood is trickling down and takes a deep breath. "I have a couple officers looking for the SUV. You two need to clear the scene, but first check to see if anything has been taken."

Josh comes in panting behind him. "I really need to do more cardio." He gulps and holds his side. "Rooms are intact. Anything taken up here?"

"May I?" I gesture to the file cabinet. Travis hands me a pair of gloves. I put them on and sift through the files. Every file is in alphabetical order based on last names. I shake my head. "Nothing appears to be missing."

Travis frowns. "So why break-in? What are they looking for?"

I bite my lip.

Josh shrugs and says, "Come on, I'm starving. How about pizza?"

"Don't you think we should call Vicky?"

"I already did. Left a message for Bethany. She's probably still at the hospital." He checks his phone. "How about I call in a pizza? We can pick it up and go to your house."

I stare at the file cabinet, trying to figure out why someone would be looking at client files.

Josh interrupts my thoughts, "Autumn?"

"Yeah sure. Sounds good," I mumble still staring at the file cabinet. "I'm going to look around a little bit more just to be sure nothing else is missing and then lock up." I turn and glance up at him.

He nods. "I'll grab the pizza then come back and pick you up." His stomach rumbles.

I smile. "You better feed that thing."

"I know. I haven't eaten since noon and..." He checks the clock on his phone. "It's almost five thirty."

I gasp.

"Don't make fun. I'm a growing man." He flexes his arm.

"Growing?" I raise an eyebrow.

He kisses his bicep. "These muscles need fuel."

"You're ridiculous." I push him toward the door. "Text me when you get back."

He salutes me and disappears.

I tuck my hands into my scrub pockets and feel the

plastic sandwich bag I put the hair tie in earlier. I take out the hair tie. Wisps of hair are caught in the tie. They look kind of red. Faded silver writing is on the inside, I squint to read it then gasp.

"Autumn? What's that?"

"Nothing." I hide it behind my back.

Travis pursues his lips. "Hiding evidence is a crime."

"I'm not hiding anything."

"Give it to me, Autumn." He holds out his hand.

I roll the tie around my fingers before reluctantly handing it to him.

He studies it for a second then his eyes grow wide. "Autumn, why do you have Cat's hair tie?"

I bite my lip.

"Where did you find this?"

I can't look at him so I study my shoes.

"Autumn, where did you get this hair tie?"

"In the blue room." I glance up at him.

He narrows his eyes at me. "When?"

"Today. It was on the rug underneath the massage table."

"Was Cat visiting you today?"

I shake my head. Tears are starting to form in my eyes.

"Was anyone else in the blue room before you?"

I shake my head again.

Silence fills the room. The only sound is the clock ticking on the wall behind me.

I sneak a peek at Travis. His face is pale and his eyes are focused on the hair tie.

"She always has one in her hair. When she kept losing them, she decided to sew her name in them. I thought it was kind of silly, but she wanted to keep track of them and avoid getting lice. Not that I can blame her for that. The morning

April died, Cat had her hair in a ponytail. When we left, her hair was down." His eyes meet mine. "Autumn," his voice is raspy.

My mind is spinning trying to think of ways the hair tie could have gotten into the blue room without Cat having killed her mother. Cat was a sweet girl. She wouldn't kill her mother, would she? It didn't make sense. What motive did she have?

"Boarding school," Travis whispers as if he read my mind. "Cat was angry about April wanting to send her away to boarding school. Told me she would make sure it didn't happen. I tried to reassure her I would fix it, but we got interrupted by the attempted break-in call. Do you think..." his words trailed off.

He looks so lost and broken, I can't take it. I move toward him and wrap my arms around his waist. Travis rests his chin on my head. His musky scent takes me right back to high school. Sneaking kisses at our lockers, holding hands down the hallway, snuggled up in the bed of his truck. It's all so familiar yet so overwhelming.

"Am I interrupting something?"

Travis drops his hands and practically shoves me away from him. I stagger back.

"Cat, what are you doing here?" Travis stuffs the hair tie in his pocket.

"We were supposed to go for pizza. Aunt Regina called and told me about the Salon so I thought I would just meet you here. She sounded like she needed some pizza too."

"You walked?" Travis runs a hand through his blond hair.

Cat nods. "I was at the library. It's only a couple blocks."

Travis nods slowly.

"Why are you at the Spa and not at the Salon?" Cat looks back and forth between me and Travis.

"Someone broke in." I clasp my hands in front of me, feeling like a teenager caught making out with her boyfriend. My cheeks are flushed and my heart is racing.

"Oh no." Cat's eyes grow wide. "Did you catch them?"

Travis shakes his head. "I think we're done here. Let's go get Aunt Regina."

"What's wrong?" Cat narrows her eyes at her father.

"Nothing's wrong." Travis's eyes go wide as if trying to convince her.

"You're acting weird."

"I'm not acting weird. Why do you think I'm acting weird? Autumn, I'm not acting weird, am I?" Travis rambles.

I purse my lips and stifle a laugh. He's so obvious. "Actually, you are. I think you should just ask her."

"Autumn, don't."

"Ask me what?" Cat tucks a strand of loose hair behind her ear. Her hair is pulled back into a short ponytail at the base of her neck. Probably with a hair tie like the one Travis is hiding in his pocket.

"Nothing."

"Travis, you-"

"Autumn, NO," he says firmly, glaring at me. "Let's go, Cat." He takes her arm and leads her to the back door.

I want to call after him. Ask Cat the questions myself, but I know I can't. It's not my place. I'll give Travis time to figure it out, but I can't let it go. If Cat did kill April, I know Travis will do anything to protect her even if it means making me the scape goat and I can't go down for this no matter how much I like Cat.

12

"She's late." I glance at the Elvis clock and tap my fork on the table.

"Quit fidgeting." Josh shoves another bite of pancake in his mouth, slurping up drops of syrup before they land on his dark gray suit.

"Do you think she'll show up?" I check my phone again then sweep a hand through my thick hair. I left it down for church, which now I'm regretting along with my wardrobe; a short black skirt with tights and a thin blue blouse. The temperatures are above freezing today, but it's still cold.

"She texted you she would meet us. It's Sunday. People either sleep in or go to church. Maybe she overslept or services went long. Most people don't get up and go to the seven am service like you make me do."

I make a face. "Successful people get up early."

"Not on Sundays. Sundays are a day of rest. So, rest, Autumn. Take a breath. You're supposed to be an example of a person who is balanced, centered and at peace."

"Says who?"

He finishes chewing and licks syrup off his lips. "I don't know. I just assume that's how we're supposed to be."

"He's right," Sally says, standing next to Josh.

I jump not realizing she's standing there. Her black hair is tied back in a bun at the base of her neck. A floral dress is clinging to her thin frame underneath a thick plushy coat and her cheeks are rosy from the cold. "Good morning." I gesture to the seat next to me.

She slides in and removes her coat.

Our blond waitress, Tiffany appears in her fifties themed uniform, poodle skirt and all to take her order.

"Nothing for me, thanks."

Tiffany nods and dashes back to the kitchen.

I open my mouth to say something, but Sally beats me to it.

"I know why you asked me here."

"You do?" I glance at Josh, who gulps down his orange juice and raises an eyebrow.

"You think I killed April."

"Well-" I look away not able to meet her eyes.

"I didn't."

"You didn't?" I study her to see if I can pick up any tells that show she's lying.

She shakes her head. "I should have."

I frown. "Why?"

"She slept with my boyfriend."

"Your boyfriend?"

"Dr. Gregory."

I gasp. "Dr. Gregory is your boyfriend."

Sally nods then shakes her head. "He was until he broke up with me...because of her."

"Dr. Gregory told me he just got out of a long-distance relationship before he moved here." I cast Josh another look. He's gaping at Sally like she's an alien. Probably as surprised as I am she's talking this much.

Sally scowls. "April recruited him. Talked him into coming here. Into bringing his expertise to this dinky town. I told him it was crazy. His skills should be used in a big city, where he can help the most people, but he came here. Why?"

I shrug. "Tired of the big city?"

"Yeah right. We love the big city. There's nothing to do here. It's so boring. If it wasn't for her, we would still be living in Chicago." Sally slaps the table.

Josh and I jump. Luckily, the café is basically empty except for old man Harry sipping his coffee at the counter. He doesn't even turn around. Probably doesn't have his hearing aids turned on. I gape at Sally. Her anger throws me. I've never seen her utter more than a few words and here she is spouting her personal baggage. "So why did you move here?"

"To get Brian to come home."

"Brian is Dr. Gregory."

Sally nods. "He's my soulmate. We were going to get married. I'd just finished massage school. It was the perfect time to get engaged except when he takes me to dinner, instead of proposing, he breaks up with me. Tells me he's moving here. It broke my heart. I cried for weeks then made a plan to get him back."

I study her to see if she's lying, but I don't think she is. "So, you moved here for him?"

She picks at a piece of chipped nail polish. "Then I saw him with her."

"Who? April?"

"Yes. They were kissing in his office when I went to take him lunch. That's when I knew. Knew she was the reason he moved here. I've spent the past few weeks researching her and I found out a bunch of stuff that could take April Biggs down or well could have."

I want to know everything she has on April, but refrain. "Did you confront April?"

"I threatened her. She offered me a ton of money to give her all the information I had on her and then told me to leave town. When I refused to leave until Brian went home with me. She ended things with Brian and gave him a big bonus to move back to Chicago, but he won't leave. Says he likes it here. Wants to set down roots. Can you believe that?"

I want to tell her I can because I love this town, but know it won't get me anywhere so I change the subject. "Did you take the money?"

"Of course, I did."

"Did you give her the file of information you had on her?"

Sally smiles, her eyes sparkle with mischief. "I gave her a copy. I still have the originals. Figured you would like to see it since you're in it."

"Me? Why am I in there?"

"You'll see." Sally digs in her bag and pulls out a file folder. "I won't charge you. You've been so nice to me. Both of you." She looks to Josh. "I'm quitting the spa. Moving back to Chicago. Brian made it very clear we were over and with the money April gave me, I can start fresh, maybe pursue something I'm actually good at."

I take the file, ready to dive into it, curiosity pushing me to open it, but I resist and smile at Sally. "Why did you become a massage therapist?"

Sally laughs. "Brian suggested it. The schooling was short, pay's good...if you have clients and I can set my own hours. It was something I could do until we had children." She sighs and her tears form in her eyes. "Guess I'll have to wait longer for that. My only dream has ever been to be a mom. I thought Brian would make that dream come true." A tear drops onto the table.

I pat her hand. "I'm so sorry, Sally."

She gives my hand a squeeze. "I'm leaving tomorrow. Bethany knows I quit. She told me Vicky was still in the hospital. Something about her breathing being erratic. I think I'll pop over and tell them both good-bye. Vicky didn't have to hire me or keep me on since I'm awful at massage, but she did. Maybe I'll see if I can catch Brian. Try and change his mind one last time." She gets up and I stand to give her a hug and so does Josh. When she leaves, I sit down and stare at the file folder.

"Well open it already." Josh reaches for the file folder.

I swat his hand away. "Not here."

"Why not?"

Before I can answer the door opens and a blast of cold air sweeps through the diner along with Travis and Cat. I slip the folder into my bag and take a sip of my tea, which is now cold. I fight back a grimace as they walk up to us.

"Good morning, Autumn. Josh. Can we join you?" Cat asks, gesturing to the seat next to me. Her red hair is pulled back in a ponytail and her long green dress is covered by a black wool coat.

I move over, but Travis shakes his head and guides Cat to the table behind us. He slides in behind Josh. His dark suit tightening around his shoulders as he picks up a menu.

Josh rolls his eyes.

I narrow mine and stare straight at the back of Travis's head. Hopefully, he'll feel the hate rolling off me. Guess he didn't question Cat about the hair tie. If he won't, I will. I turn my attention to Josh. "What color was that hair tie we found in the massage room yesterday?" I raise my voice so

Cat can hear me over the 50's music floating through the café.

Josh smirks. "I think it was blue."

I nod and sneak a peek at Cat. She's focusing on the menu, but I see her sneak a glance at me. Good she heard me. Josh got all the details last night over pizza and was ready to knock down Travis's door to get answers. My dad is still making his way slowly through the snow storms, which keep popping up around the Midwest. He's stuck in Oklahoma and isn't sure when he'll be here. Josh is determined to keep me out of jail in the meantime even if it means sending Cat to jail. I shudder at the thought. Surely, this is all a misunderstanding. "There was some writing in it too. A name. Do you remember the name on it?"

Travis clears his throat loudly. Oh, like that's not obvious.

"Something with a c." He rubs his chin as if trying to come up with the name.

I bite my lip to hold back a laugh.

"You found my hair tie, didn't you?" Cat said, slapping down her menu.

Travis turns and glares at me. "We did. I was planning to talk to you about it later."

"We can talk now." Cat gets up and slides in next to Josh then waits for her father to join us.

He slowly gets out of the booth. His chest rising and falling as if he's taking deep breaths to calm himself down before sitting down next to me.

Tiffany rushes out and takes their order. For the café being empty she sure seems busy. She disappears back into the kitchen then returns with coffee and orange juice before skittering off again.

Travis places his arms on the table and clasps his hands.

He takes another deep breath, but before he can say anything his cell phone rings and so does mine. We give each other a look then dig for our phones both turning our backs to each other as we answer.

"Autumn, something awful has happened. Can you come to the hospital?" Bethany sniffs into the phone.

"Sure. What happened?" My heart thumping a million miles an hour and my brain racing with scenarios.

"I've got to go, but please hurry." The line goes dead.

I stare down at the phone then turn to Travis. His face is pale and he's murmuring into the phone.

"What is it?"

"Bethany wants us to come to the hospital. Something bad has happened, but she wouldn't give me any details. I hope Vicky's ok."

Josh finishes his juice and tosses some cash on the table.

Travis hangs up and tosses some more money on the table. "I have to go."

"Why? What happened?" Cat asks, reaching for her coat.

"There's been another murder."

"Murder!" Josh and I say in unison.

I would usually call out Jinx and he owes me a massage, but Travis's words have me stunned. "Who?"

Travis stands and puts on his coat, avoiding my eyes.

I scoot out after him and shrug into my coat. "Bethany just called me and told me to come to the hospital. Is it Vicky? Did something happen?

He takes a sip of his coffee before clearing his throat and finally meeting my eyes. "Yes."

13

I'm numb. People are talking and moving around me, but I can't process any of it. My boss is dead. Not to mention a friend. Vicky gave both me and Josh a job fresh out of massage school. She took a chance on us and I hope never regretted it. Everyone loved Vicky. Who would do this?

"Here, drink this." Josh hands me a bottle of water then sits down next to me in the hospital waiting room.

I unscrew the lid and toss back the water. The cool liquid feels good on my dry throat. "How did this happen?"

"Travis is still asking questions. Gathering evidence. I overheard one of the nurses say they found her with a pillow over her face. Someone must have smothered her in her sleep."

I gasp. "How awful. Who would do something like that? More importantly why?"

Josh drops his head into his hands. I know he's upset. Vicky was so nice to both of us. She especially loved Josh. He was her favorite. The son she never had. Josh wipes his eyes and lifts his head. "Bethany is beside herself. I took her some water, but she's inconsolable. Blames herself. Says she stepped out to get something to eat and when she came back...she found her mother."

"Poor thing. She has no one. Her father died when she was just a baby and now her mother's gone." I shake my head and swallow the lump forming in my throat. "Where were the nurses? Did anyone see anything?"

"It was during a shift change. Vicky was at the end of the hall, right by the fire exit, which is conveniently broken. It would be easy for someone to slip in and slip out unnoticed."

"Do you think the murder is connected to the break-in or April's murder?"

"Maybe, but I don't see how those two are connected."

I frown. "None of this makes any sense." I pause. "We need to go over the suspect list for April's murder."

"Again?" Josh groans.

"Yes, again. Our boss and friend was just murdered. I think her murder and April's are somehow connected. Not to mention Bethany may be in danger. We need to solve this and fast."

"At least they can't pin this murder on you." Josh mumbles.

I give him a look that says I don't find him amusing. I glance around to be sure no one is listening. The waiting room is empty except for Cat listening to her iPod in the corner, earbuds tucked in tightly. Surely, she can't hear me, but I keep my voice low. "Bobby, Nikki, Sally, the Mayor, Dr. Gregory, Vicky, Cat."

"Vicky's out because well..."

I grimace. "I don't like to speak ill of the dead, but what if Vicky killed April?"

Josh cringes. "I can't go there right now."

"Fine. We'll put Vicky on the maybe list." I pause and regroup then say. "I'm going to take Bobby and Nikki off the list."

"Why?"

"One Bobby didn't know about the affair." I hold up my index finger and begin counting. "Two, he wasn't at the spa and three, he seemed relatively happy with his life with April."

"Okay fine, let's take Bobby off the list." Josh sighs as if relieved.

I continue. "Nikki was at the spa, had motive, but was also going to get some money from April in exchange for her silence about the affair so why kill April before getting the money? It doesn't make sense."

"Revenge? Sometimes sweeter than money?"

I shake my head. "Nikki had plans for that money. Also, she's a yogi. They are all about peace and harmony. Killing is not that."

He nods. "Fine, Nikki's out. Who's next?"

I glance around the room again to be sure no one is listening then lean into Josh. "Sally. She was blackmailing April and was at the spa. Not to mention April insulted her massage and slept with her boyfriend. Stole her dream of getting married and having babies. It's a pretty strong motive."

"But April paid her off."

"So?"

"So, it's not like she got nothing. Why kill April?"

"To make her really pay."

Josh doesn't look convinced, but says, "So, Sally stays on the list?"

"For now."

He sighs and leans forward, bracing his forearms on his

knees and rolling the water bottle back and forth in his hands. "Who's next?"

"The Mayor."

"He wasn't at the spa and April's his daughter."

"True, but the Mayor also loves money and his reputation means everything to him. April cut him off. He was broke. Desperate."

"Bobby said April found out something about her father."

I bite my lip. "We need to find out more about the Mayor. He stays on the list."

Josh nods.

"That brings us to Dr. Gregory. He was having an affair with April. She broke it off. He could have been angry. Killed her in a lover's rage."

"But he wasn't at the spa."

"Good point. What if he broke in? Hid somewhere and slipped in and out unnoticed."

Josh gives me a look. "Travis was in the break room the whole time. There's only two exits and you and Bethany were standing by the other one. I doubt he killed April."

I stick out my lower lip and pout. "Fine. We'll take Dr. Gregory off."

"What about Travis?"

"Travis?"

"You had him on the list after the funeral. April was threatening to send Cat to boarding school. He was at the spa."

"I don't think Travis killed April," I say softly.

Josh frowns. "Because you know for a fact he didn't kill April or because you don't want to believe he's capable of murder?"

I don't answer. Josh will flip out if I tell him I'm having

feelings for Travis again. I'm not even ready to admit them to myself let alone anyone else. I mean the man cheated on me, broke my heart, hasn't talked to me in fifteen years and now, I'm a suspect in his investigation. It shouldn't bring on the warm fuzzy feelings yet I can't stop thinking about him. I do know in my gut he didn't kill April, but I need to stay objective. "Fine, we'll keep Travis on the list."

Josh smiles as if he's won a prize.

My stomach churns and bile burns my throat. The thought of Travis killing someone shakes me to the core. It's unfathomable. It's the same feeling I get when I think of myself killing someone. The whole thing seems wrong.

"What about Cat?" Josh nods toward the teen in the corner.

I sigh and turn my gaze toward her. Did Cat kill her mother? Evidence is pointing that way. She was at the spa. Knew her mother was there. She admitted to seeing her SUV. Told her father she would make sure she didn't get sent to boarding school. Her hair tie was found at the scene of the crime. All signs point to Cat.

Cat looks up and smiles. She takes out her ear buds and walks over to us. "Can I join you?"

"Sure."

She takes the seat next to me.

I'm not sure what to ask. She's a minor. Her dad's a detective. I need to tread lightly. If Travis finds out Cat admits to murder in front of me, he'll find a way to turn it around and convince the judge I persuaded her somehow. I know Travis. I know how he thinks. He'll do anything to protect the people he loves. A prang of hurt sears my heart. Emotional scars take time to heal...sometimes they never do. I know in my heart Travis will protect Cat to the ends of the earth. Me on the other hand, I'm not sure.

"I didn't kill my mom," Cat says quietly.

I don't respond. Saying nothing sometimes works better than asking questions. Makes the person want to talk to fill in the silence.

"I was in the spa. My dad let me in the back door. I had to use the restroom. Too many hot chocolates at breakfast." She smiles up at me.

I smile back, but still don't say anything.

"When I was in the restroom, I heard my dad's phone ring. He answered then I heard the backdoor open and the room went silent. I washed my hands and as I was getting ready to open the door, I heard Vicky mumbling about my mom. Then I heard the sound of metal scraping against wood then silence. I stepped out and spotted Sally sitting in Vicky's office. She was busy on the computer so I went back into the break room. I was about ready to leave when I heard Vicky stomping down the hallway. She was muttering to herself then she disappeared into her office. Next thing I know, you're shouting for help. I rushed out to get my dad, but couldn't find him. I went back inside and heard you say my mom's name so I made my way to the front of the spa. Bethany was on the phone with the 911 operator, Aunt Regina was comforting you on the couch so I thought I would go see if my mom was ok." Cat sniffles. A tear drops onto her hand. "The door to the blue room was open. I peeked in and saw my mom. I thought it was a joke at first. Like someone was pranking me. I went in and shook her. She wouldn't wake up. I must have lost my hair tie when I was shaking her." She runs a hand over her short ponytail. "My hair is so short, mom wouldn't let me grow it out and I hate having it in my face, it doesn't take much for my hair ties to come out. That's why I sewed my name into them because I'm always losing them and mom kept getting upset every time she had to buy new ones." She gives me a shy smile.

I smile back, trying not to roll my eyes at April's pettiness. Hair ties are cheap and April was loaded. What kind of mother gets upset about hair ties when she drops $500 on shoes? I'll never understand April. I reach out and squeeze Cat's hand. "What did you do next?"

Cat sniffles again and more tears fall down her cheeks. "I got some blood on my hands so I went to the bathroom to wash them." Then she glances around. "I saw Vicky and Sally in her office. They were talking in hushed tones, but I swear I heard Vicky say, 'She's gone now'."

I gasp, but before I can say anything Travis is by Cat's side.

"How dare you." His eyes are hard and full of venom. If looks could kill I would be dead right now.

Cat pops up from her chair and rushes over to her dad before coming to my defense. "She didn't. I told her. Everything. I should have told you first, but I was scared. I think Vicky killed mom," she whispers then breaks down into sobs.

A gasp comes from behind us. "No, she didn't," Bethany cries.

We all turn around to find her standing there shaking like she's been out in the cold too long. Her face is pale, dark circles rim her eyes, her brown braid is a mess and her black scrubs are wrinkled and look like she slept in them. I stand and hug Bethany. "I'm so sorry about your mom."

She hugs me for a moment then glares at Cat. "How dare you say my mother killed yours."

Cat sniffles and hiccups. "I-I heard her."

"But you didn't see her kill your mother, did you?"

"Well...no." Cat hiccups again.

"You have no proof. For all we know, you're trying to blame my mother to get away with killing yours."

We all gasp.

I know Bethany is grieving, but this is wrong on so many levels yet could she be right? I glance over at Cat, her face is red and blotchy, tears are still streaming down her cheeks as she sobs into Travis's chest. Travis is shooting daggers at Bethany with his eyes as he pats Cat on the back. Is Cat trying to blame Vicky since she's dead? Using the whole dead woman tell no tales angle. Vicky can't defend herself so it would make it easy to blame her, but then the real question is who killed Vicky? Sally? If Cat really heard Sally and Vicky talking about April 'being gone' maybe they were working together. Sally is leaving town and came over to visit Vicky and Bethany before she left; maybe she killed Vicky to ensure she wouldn't rat on her. Speaking of Sally, where is she? I glance around the waiting room, but don't see her. My eyes land on Bethany and I ask, "Did Sally come by?"

Bethany crosses her arms and nods, still glaring at Cat says, "She went to see Dr. Gregory." I open my mouth to offer to get her some tea when she says, "I'm not going to stand here and listen to this nonsense." She sneers at Cat turns on her heels and stomps from the room.

I stare after her in shock. I've never heard Bethany raise her voice or act like this. She's always been quiet and sweet. I guess I would be upset too if someone accused my mother of murder. I won't hold it against her. She just lost her mother.

Josh clears his throat and I glance over at him. He motions for me to follow him.

Travis quirks an eyebrow. I mouth "Cafeteria" and he nods.

Josh leads me down the hallway. Neither of us speaking. I think we're both still shell shocked by everything we just heard.

"Do you think Vicky killed April?" Josh shivers.

The smell of disinfectant hits me as we turn a corner. "I don't know. It sure sounds like it. If Vicky killed April then who killed Vicky?"

He gives me a look. I know what he's thinking, we're both thinking it as we run into a familiar dark-haired friend.

"Sally."

"Isn't it awful?" Her eyes are blood shot and there are tear streaks are on her cheeks. "I can't believe Vicky is dead."

I exchange a look with Josh. He frowns. I turn back to Sally. "Did you get a chance to see her before she died?"

Sally shakes her head. "I showed up right after. Bethany had just found her."

I exchange a look with Josh. Seems a little too convenient.

Dr. Gregory comes up behind Sally and wraps his arms around her tiny waist then kisses the top of her head before looking at us. "I'm sorry to hear about your boss. The security around here is awful. Sometimes I think working in Chicago was safer. At least we had guards on staff."

"That's why we're moving back, honey," Sally leans back into his chest.

"Honey?" I try to keep the level of surprise out of my voice.

Sally sniffles then smiles. "I've talked Brian into coming back to Chicago with me. We're going to give our relationship another shot."

I'm speechless. I must look like a deer in headlights because Josh nudges me in the ribs. "Well...that's unexpected."

He nudges me harder.

"I mean...Congratulations?" I say it more like a question than a statement. I'm totally confused. Didn't Sally just tell us at breakfast Brian or Dr. Gregory was planning to stay here?

Sally wipes her eyes then takes Brian's hand. "We're leaving right after Vicky's funeral whenever that will be. Hopefully, before the end of the week." She wraps her free hand around Brian's arm and puts her head on his shoulder before looking at us. "We're going to grab some coffee and check on Bethany. Want to join us?"

"No. Thank you."

They nod and walk off.

I watch them walk away hand in hand. "What just happened?"

Josh shrugs. "Beats me."

"I thought Dr. Gregory was staying here."

"Love makes you do crazy things."

"Or murder does."

14

"I'm closing the spa for the week." Bethany's voice is shaky as she taps on the computer keys. "I have so much to do before the funeral on Thursday." It's Monday and we're huddled around the receptionist desk. "There's not enough time to get everything done in between working here and planning Mom's-", her voice breaks off and tears spill from her eyes.

I move around the desk and pull her into a hug.

She gives me a squeeze then steps back, wipes her eyes and says, "I'm sorry. I know you both need the hours."

"We're good. You take care of you this week and let us know if we can help with any arrangements." Josh pats Bethany on the shoulder.

She smiles up at him and nods.

"Do you need us to reschedule any clients?" I turn toward the desk to see what she's been working on. Josh and I are a little concerned Bethany will close the spa. She's young. Only twenty-one. She doesn't have much business experience. Her mom was grooming her to take over, but she's nowhere near ready to take on everything that goes with running a spa. Our jobs could be in jeopardy.

Bethany toys with the end of her braid and stares blankly at the computer screen. "I sent out a mass email to all the clients last night informing them of mother's passing although everyone probably already knows, but I included the funeral details and told them we would be closed this week. I'm going to finish up some paperwork then head to the funeral home. You two can go. I want to be alone."

Josh and I exchange a look. Something seems off with Bethany. I know she just lost her mother, but she seems like she's in shock.

"Are you sure everything is ok?"

Bethany blinks then focuses on me. "I'm fine. Why?"

"You seem...well...not yourself."

She blinks again. "My mother just died. I don't know how to run a business. I don't know how to do anything. She did everything. I'm lost without her," She drops her head in her hands and sobs.

I bend down and give her another hug. "We'll help you, Bethany. We're a team." I look to Josh for support.

"Autumn's right. We're a team. The spa is in good hands. Nothing has to change." He pats Bethany's shoulder again.

"Everything has changed. I don't know if I can do this."

"Do what?" I ask, a sinking feeling forming in my gut.

"The spa. I'm not sure I can keep it open." Bethany bursts into another round of tears.

She sobs onto my shoulder, soaking my black scrub top. Several minutes pass which seem like hours. My knees start to wobble and feel about to give out. I need to get up, but don't want to seem insensitive. I pray she's almost done, but don't want to rush her.

"I'm sorry, guys." Bethany lifts her head and wipes her eyes.

Josh hands her a tissue as I stand up.

She takes the tissue, blows her nose then stares at us. "I'm not prepared to make any decisions right now. That's another reason I want to close the spa. I need time to wrap my mind around things."

"Of course. We totally understand." I reach out and squeeze her shoulder. "We'll leave you to your work and check in later. Call if you need anything."

Bethany nods and turns back to the computer.

I follow Josh from the room as I glance around the spa. The chipping white paint, green tile, framed pictures of hot stones and palm trees line the walls. This place has been my second home for the past ten years. The thought of it closing makes my stomach and my heart hurt. I sigh and run a hand through my ponytail. Static crackles and shocks my fingers.

Josh is putting on his coat in the break room as I pass by. He catches me eye and I nod toward the office. He narrows his eyes and shakes his head. We talked about this plan last night. Check out Vicky's computer to see if she has anything incriminating on it or anything linking her to April's murder. We were going to wait until the spa was empty, but time is of the essence. If Sally was in on April's murder and killed Vicky, she's going to skip town and get away with murder.

"What are you doing?" Josh hisses, following me.

"Checking out Vicky's computer."

"Now?"

"Yes, now. Cover for me."

He crosses his arms and gives me a disapproving look.

I ignore him. "If Bethany comes back tell her I went to

the bathroom. I'll turn on the fan and the light so it looks like I'm in there. If she tries to go to the office turn on some Josh Parker charm and distract her and talk loudly so I can hear you."

He gives me a doubtful look. "This is a bad idea. Why don't we come back once Bethany's gone?"

"It will look suspicious and we can't let Sally get away with murder. Vicky's computer may have something on it."

He sighs and retreats to the break room.

I'm glad he doesn't fight me on this. He can be really stubborn especially when it comes to my safety. That's what best friends are for, right? I head toward the office at the end of the hall. The bathroom is directly across from it so it will be easy to make it look like I'm in the bathroom. Thankfully, the door to the office is open. Even Vicky's computer is on and there's no password. That's a relief.

The usual files are on the desktop. I click into the 'Files' tab and nothing abnormal shows up. Maybe I'm on the wrong path. I sigh and move to get up when my scrub pants snag on something. Shoot. These are my favorite pants. I check my pants, it's only a little tear. I can probably sew it shut. Then I go in search of the culprit. Protect another pair of innocent pants from its jagged clutches.

I run a hand down the side of the desk and find the piece of the desk sticking out. I try to push it in and it pops out. It's a secret compartment. I slide out the secret drawer and pull out a file folder.

"Josh, what are you still doing here?"

"Autumn had to use the restroom," He replies, loudly.

Shoot, I need to get out of here. I stuff the folder back in the compartment when a photo slips out and floats to the floor. I gasp. Frozen in place. I can't seem to tear my eyes away from the couple in front of me.

"She should be out any minute. The hospital food must have upset her stomach." Josh stomps his foot on the ground. "Did you see that spider?"

"A spider? Where? Mom said she had the place sprayed for bugs. I hate spiders," Bethany whines.

"Stand on the chair and I'll kill it," Josh orders, even louder.

"Spiders don't have ears, Josh. You don't have to yell."

I scoop up the photo and shove it back in the file folder. I'll come back for it once Bethany's gone. Once the secret compartment is in place, I slip across the hall and into the bathroom. My heart is racing and I'm shaking. The picture is forever burned in my mind. I turn on the water and splash some cool water on my face then take a deep breath and shut off the light. I almost collide with Bethany as I walk out. "Sorry, didn't see you there."

"Are you alright?"

My palms are sweaty and my heart is beating like a drum in my chest. "Some tummy issues. A little too much cafeteria food last night."

She raises an eyebrow, but nods. "Well I hope you feel better. I'm getting ready to lock up and head to the funeral home."

"Do you need any help? We'd be happy to go with you." I smile and pray it's reaching my eyes. The picture is flipping through my mind. Josh is going to freak out when I tell him.

"No. I've got it. Thank you though." Bethany continues to stare at me with a weird expression on her face. Am I sweating? I feel like I'm sweating.

"You look kind of flushed. Are you sure you're not coming down with something?"

I raise a hand to my forehead. It is kind of warm, but I was almost caught snooping in my dead boss's office.

"Maybe some food poisoning. I should probably go home and lie down."

Bethany nods and gives me a once over when my stomach growls. I place a hand over it as she glances down. "Hope you feel better soon."

"Thanks. Call if you need anything." I hurry down the hall and practically plow into Josh. He's holding my coat. "We need to leave, now." I slip on my jacket and move toward the back door.

"What's going on?"

"Tell you in the car."

"Oh, Autumn," Bethany calls from the hallway.

Shoot. Did she figure out I was in the office? "Yes." I whip around, holding my breath and feeling like I may faint.

She pops her head around the corner and studies me for a moment before saying, "Peppermint tea should help soothe your belly."

I let out the breath I'm holding and smile at her. "I'll be sure to pick some up. Thanks, Bethany."

"Feel better," she coos.

I push open the back door and into the bitter cold air. Out of the corner of my eye I see a black SUV parked in the back of the parking lot. Someone is inside. "Get in the Jeep, now." I tug on Josh's hand and pull him toward the Jeep, trying not to seem too obvious. I hear an engine start up. Once we're in the Jeep I feel a little safer, but we need to get out of here. "Drive."

"Autumn, what's going on?"

"Ask later. Drive now."

Josh doesn't question me anymore and pulls out of the parking lot. I check the rearview mirror. The dark SUV pulls out a few minutes behind us. I watch to see if it turns off, but it doesn't. "Take the next right."

"I thought we were going home."

"Just do it," I snap. I should feel guilty, but my adrenaline is pumping. "Someone is following us."

Josh checks the mirror. "Is that a dark SUV?"

"Pretty sure."

"Do you think it's the same one that tried to run you over?"

"Maybe. Just keep making turns, but don't speed up. Make it look like we're headed somewhere."

"Where are we headed?"

"Let's drive around for a bit and if they're still following us, let's go to the police station."

"You're the boss." Josh makes another turn. The tires squeal slightly on the wet surface. Luckily, the roads are clear, but they're still wet, which could make driving dangerous in these cold temperatures. At least it's above freezing. He makes another turn. "We're headed out of town, Autumn. I'm not going to be able to circle back to the police station without turning around somewhere."

I check the rearview mirror. We're still being followed. "Turn off at Harrington's Farm. We'll make it look like we're going to buy some furniture."

"Furniture?"

"Yes, I need a new end table by the front door."

"You do?"

"No, but we can make it look like I do if push comes to shove. Just pull into the drive and veer off on one of the side paths leading to the barn. If they follow, keep driving. If not, we can turn around and go back home."

Josh makes another turn. His jaw is clenched and he's focused on the road. He keeps gripping and un-gripping the steering wheel. I know he's nervous; so am I. "We must be getting close to solving this murder, otherwise they wouldn't be following us."

"A lot of good that does us if we're the next victims," he mumbles and checks the rearview mirror again.

I bite my lip. I hadn't thought of that. Are they following us to kill us? "The Harrington Farm is up ahead on the right. Don't turn on your blinker."

Josh whips into the driveway and pulls onto a path off to the side. We both turn around to see if they follow us. The dark SUV drives by without turning in. I let out the breath I've been holding and see Josh exhale too. Then we look at each other and laugh. "Are we paranoid or were they really following us?"

"Better safe than sorry." He reverses the Jeep and heads back to town.

I keep checking the rearview mirror, but no one's following us. "I'm starving. Let's stop at the café for lunch."

"Sounds good to me. I've been craving a BLT since breakfast."

"It's only noon."

"What can I say. Food is always on my mind." He winks at me.

I roll my eyes then remember the photos. "I found something interesting in Vicky's office."

Josh pulls into the café parking lot. It's full since it's lunch time. He finds a spot in the back and parks. "What did you find?"

"I didn't get a chance to look in the folder, but a picture fell out."

"A picture of what?"

"You mean of who?"

Josh rolls his eyes. "Autumn, what did you find?"

"A picture of—" Before I can answer there's a knock on my window. I jump and turn.

"I need to talk to you." Travis's eyes are narrowed and his jaw is clenched.

I want to ignore him. He's been a jerk, but I shouldn't have let Cat talk to me without Travis present. I sigh and unbuckle my seatbelt. "I'll meet you inside."

"You don't have to talk to him." Josh glares over my shoulder at Travis.

I shake my head and say softly, "Yes, I do."

Josh scoffs and shoves open the car door.

I step out into the cold and button up my coat before stuffing my hands in my pockets.

"Do you want me to order you anything?" Josh calls from the front of the Jeep.

"Same as you."

He smiles at me then shoots Travis a piercing glare before heading inside the café.

I want to follow him. The old fifties themed diner looks lively and inviting. I can even see Tiffany bouncing from table to table in her poodle skirt. Snow blows across the parking lot. I shiver and huddle against the Jeep to shield myself from the wind.

Travis steps closer to me. I refuse to look at him. He does smell really good though. Woodsy with a hint of oranges. I close my eyes and drink him in.

"Cat told me everything." His breath is minty and hot on my cheek.

My mind goes to mush and I almost forget what Cat told me yesterday. "She did?" I give in and look up at him as snow begins to fall lightly around us. To anyone else we probably appear to be a couple in love except we're not. We're discussing murder.

He nods. "I took her down to the station. The Captain got her statement. We have Bethany down there now to see if she knew anything about April's murder or if her mother acted alone."

"So, you think Vicky killed April?"

"Based on what Cat heard it sounds like it."

I frown. "Who killed Vicky?"

Travis looks around the parking lot. "I'm not supposed to be sharing this with civilians, but we have a warrant out for Sally and Dr. Gregory."

"Why?"

"We think they acted together with Vicky to kill April. Vicky killed April then to make sure Vicky doesn't rat on them, Sally or Dr. Gregory killed Vicky and they're each other's alibi."

My head is spinning. "What's the motives?"

"Bobby told me April wanted to open another spa in town. It would have sunk Vicky. He also said April was bullying Sally about her bad massages and Dr. Gregory was having an affair with April. She ended it, he didn't want to end it. Revenge. I think he's the one who's been breaking into the spa."

"For what reason?"

Travis shrugs. "Maybe the original plan was for Dr. Gregory to kill April, but when you scared him away, Vicky decided to kill her. Sally was her alibi."

I gasp. "She was?"

He nods. "She said she and Vicky were working on advertising in the office."

"Where did Sally go after you questioned her?"

He frowns. "What do you mean?"

"I mean I didn't see Sally at the spa after April was killed."

"I questioned her in the office. I assumed she was still in there."

I rack my brain trying to remember the day April was murdered. I didn't go into the office so it's possible. "Why would Dr. Gregory come back and try to break into the spa again?"

"Take the focus off Vicky. Make her look like the victim."

"But why break into the spa after Vicky was already in the hospital?"

Travis opens his mouth and then shuts it again. "I don't know. I'll have to ask him when we interrogate him."

I nod. Travis doesn't know half of what's going on in this town. I think I'll keep it that way for a little while longer. I still need to look over the file Sally gave me. The thought of April having something on me turns my stomach. I was too exhausted and maybe a little scared to look last night, but now I know I have too. It could have more pieces to the puzzle.

Travis steps a little closer and reaches out to rub a hand up my arm. The touch sends electricity down my arm. "You're awful quiet. Anything you want to share?"

"Maybe later. My lunch is probably ready." I start toward the café.

He steps in my way. "Autumn..." He pauses. "I'm sorry."

My mouth drops open. "For what?"

Travis smirks then runs a hand thru his hair. "For the last fifteen years and this past week."

I blink. Not knowing what to say.

"I can't believe it's taken fifteen years to talk to you. To touch you. To be near you and when I get the chance I keep messing it up. Accusing you of murder. Yelling at you for talking to Cat. Giving you the cold shoulder. You name it, I've done it this past week. I never thought I'd get a chance to explain things. To make this right." He motions back and forth between us.

I'm stunned. My mouth starts collecting snowflakes from hanging open so long.

"Autumn, food's ready," Josh calls from the steps of the diner.

I glance up. Tears are falling down my cheeks before I even realize it. Josh must have seen them because he comes storming across the parking lot.

"What did you say to her?" He places a protective arm around my shoulder.

"Nothing that pertains to you," Travis snaps.

Josh balls his fists. "If it has to do with Autumn, it does pertain to me."

"You don't own her. She's not yours to protect."

"She's not yours either."

Travis steps back as if he's been slapped then he balls his fists and narrows his eyes at Josh. Before he can take a step toward him, I place a hand on his chest. He blinks and stares down at me.

"We'll talk later, okay."

He covers my hand with his. "You have my number." Gives my hand a squeeze before shooting Josh a glare and stomping off to his SUV.

"What was that?"

I stuff my hands in my coat and head inside without answering. The café is warm and cozy. I see our usual booth in the back with our lunches waiting for us. Hopefully, the bacon's still warm. I slide in and shed my coat.

"Autumn, what's going on?" Josh slides in across from me and pins me with a look.

I bite into my sandwich. This isn't a topic I want to discuss with Josh. He'll flip out. Fifteen years and he's been the only man in my life. Sure, I've dated, but nothing ever lasted. Mostly because they felt threatened by mine and Josh's relationship. I take another bite and try to figure out how to tell my best friend I'm thinking about giving Travis another chance. Not as in dating again. I'm not ready for that, but we could at least be on talking terms. Maybe go out as friends. Take Cat to a movie or ice skating. Friends do those things, right?

"Autumn, put down the sandwich and talk to me." Josh's leg is bouncing up and down underneath the table. Something he does when he's nervous.

I do as he asks and swallow my food. "Travis was apologizing."

"For what?"

"Everything."

"Everything?"

I nod.

"So...what does that mean?"

I shrug.

"You're not going to date him again, are you? The man's spent the last week accusing you of murder." He says the murder word a little too loud and a few people glance our way. I smile and wave and they go back to eating.

I lean forward and lower my voice, "Why don't you just put up a billboard sign if you're going to shout it from the rooftops?"

Josh cringes. "Sorry. I'm upset. I don't understand. The man cheated on you. Had a baby with another woman. With April. Your best friend at the time."

I feel like he just punched me in the gut, but I don't let him see how much he hurt me. I know he's looking out for me. "You've always been my best friend."

His worried expression softens. "Your best 'girl' friend."

I sigh. "Josh, it's been fifteen years, don't you think it's time to forgive and move on?"

He crosses his arms over his chest. "No. What he did to you...the pain he caused you...I spent weeks, no, months picking up the pieces of your broken heart." He drops his head then shakes it. "Hearing you cry yourself to sleep every night on the phone with me, you didn't smile, barely ate, didn't go out, you became a shell of the Autumn I know and love. He destroyed you. It wasn't until we left for massage school that you started to be yourself again. I won't stand by and let you fall right back into his charming trap."

"You won't let me?" I can feel the blood pounding in my ears. Everything Josh is saying is true, but it's my life. My choice. Not his.

He scoffs. "You know what I mean."

"Obviously, I don't." I raise my voice to get my point across.

"Autumn, Travis isn't right for you. You have to know that."

"He was drunk, Josh."

Josh blinks. "Travis never drank in high school."

"I know."

"So, why did he?"

"I haven't had a chance to ask him yet."

"It still doesn't excuse his behavior. He made the choice to drink. To keep drinking. To sleep with April. Nothing changes that."

My hands are shaking and I'm on the verge of tossing this sandwich in my best friend's face. "I'm gonna go."

"What? Why? Where?" His eyes are wide and he's looking at me like I'm speaking a different language.

I stand and slip on my coat. Tiffany walks by and I hand her a twenty. "Keep the change."

She looks back and forth between me and Josh before hurrying off.

"Autumn, please sit down." He grabs my wrist.

I shake him off. "I want to be alone."

"But we drove together."

"Walking in the freezing cold sounds a lot better than riding anywhere with you. Park my Jeep in my driveway when you get home."

"Autumn, please," Josh begs.

I can feel the crack in our relationship grow wider as I walk toward the door. Maybe I should go sit back down so we can talk this out. Then we can go back to my house and watch Netflix, but I can't go back. I can only go forward. Alone.

15

Why did I think this was a good idea? My nose is practically frost bit. I move it to get some sort of feeling in it. My wool coat is doing little to ward off the bitter wind. Of course, I stomped out into the cold without water proof boots. My feet and toes are aching and my fingers are like icicles hanging from my hands. At least it stopped snowing. Not that it's helping my current state.

I groan as I think of my toasty fireplace, all ready and waiting for me in my cozy little yellow house. My anger gets the best of me sometimes and makes me do erratic things like storm off into a winter wonderland.

I know Josh is probably driving around looking for me. Of course, he probably turned right out of the café. Thinking I was going to walk home, which is only two miles from the Eddie's Fifties Café, but I didn't. No, I went left. Away from town. Away from passing vehicles. Away from anyone who could help me if the mysterious dark SUV decides to abduct me or worse...

The wind kicks up and I hunker down in my coat, tucking my nose beneath the flap. A crow calls out from the cemetery gate. I shiver. Not from the cold although I'm freezing, but because cemeteries freak me out. I mean they're worse than funerals. The thought of being buried six feet under in a stuffy box for all eternity. I shiver again. I know when you're dead, your spirit moves on, hopefully to heaven, but still the thought of worms, insects, snakes...I shiver again...eating away at the flesh. My stomach turns. Time to think of something else.

I stop at the gates and peer out onto the sea of headstones. Each one lined up perfectly with the one next to it. Like soldiers standing at attention. I spot a gray-haired man in a black trench coat hovered next to a tombstone. His back is to me, but his shoulders are shaking up and down. He must be grief stricken. I tilt my head and try to see his face. Then it hits me, it's the Mayor.

His wife, father and mother are buried next to April. He must have come to visit her grave. It's been a week since she was murdered. The poor man must be beside himself. Cat is the only family he has left. Of course, he does still have his son-in-law, Bobby, but I never thought those two were very close.

I step thru the gates and for some reason feel like I'm being watched. The air around me stills and the hairs on the back of my neck stand up. I glance around, but don't see anyone. My mind must be playing tricks on me. It's probably just because I'm in a graveyard. The whole spooky ghosts, wandering spirits and haunting stories I've heard over the years. There's nothing to be afraid of...except maybe the Mayor.

"Hello, Autumn," Mayor Rollins says, not taking his eyes off April's tombstone.

"Good afternoon." I keep my distance, but can still read the headstone. April Biggs. April 1st, 1983-January 4th, 2018. Beloved Daughter, Wife and Mother. I notice Bobby didn't have his name on the stone. Usually husbands and wives are buried next to each other. It is a family plot, maybe the Mayor didn't buy a space for him. That had to be an awkward conversation.

"What can I do for you, Miss Fisher?" He turns toward me. His breath smells of coffee and onions.

I hold back a cringe. I hate the smell of onions and being called 'Miss'. It reminds me I'm thirty-three and single. No ring on my finger. No husband to go home to. No little kids running around my feet. I push the thoughts away and focus on what I need to find out...everything. "I'm sorry for your loss."

He grunts. "Are you?"

The comment makes me pause. He's trying to throw me. Steer me away from my objective. "I am. April and I were friends...once. Best friends..." I trail off. "I never wanted to see her...not like this."

He nods. "Me neither. Although I can't say I'm surprised. Everyone in town resented her. Were jealous of her. She was everything they weren't. Beautiful. Talented. Smart. Rich. She had everything."

I hold my tongue. It's not worth correcting him. Let him think...believe what he wants. Romanticize his daughter's character. He's grieving.

"You hated her too. She stole the one thing you loved the most."

I frown.

He laughs. "Travis wasn't good enough for April. I told her so when I saw her kissing him at that party. She slept with him to get back at me. It had nothing to do with you."

I snort.

"What? You don't believe me."

I shake my head. "April wanted Travis from the day he went from geek to quarterback. She had a huge crush on him our freshman year of high school. When he asked me out our junior year, I told him 'no'. It wasn't until April insisted I go out with him that I finally did. She was my best friend, I told her I wouldn't date him if she still liked him. April told me she didn't...guess she lied."

"She did that a lot."

"Lied?"

"Lied. Stole. Blackmailed. Cheated. Bought her way through life. Just like me. April's dead because of me."

I gasp not sure I heard him right. "W-what do you mean?"

"April died because she found out something I did. Something I regret doing many years ago." He hangs his head. "Something I've been trying to hide for years. Trying to make right. I never could. Probably never will."

I'm not sure what to say or what to do. My mouth is hanging open again. I have so many questions on the tip of my tongue, but before I can ask any the Mayor is lunging at me. My hands go up in defense, but don't do any good. I wasn't ready for the attack. I mentally prepare myself, my body tenses and prepares for impact.

We go down with a thud. My lower back taking the brunt of the fall. Pain shoots up my hip. I push at him, but he doesn't move. I hold my breath thinking he's going to strangle me. Stab me. Bash my head against a grave stone. What?

Nothing happens.

His breathing is short and raspy like he's winded. His

expensive cologne is making me gag. A heavy mix of spices. What is going on? Then I hear it.

Another pop. I heard the sound before he took me down.

The Mayor groans.

Tires squeal in the distance. Another pop sounds from the road. Is it a car back firing? I turn my head in time to see a dark SUV. Another pop sounds before the SUV speeds off.

Something sticky is caking my hands. I push on the Mayor's chest. It's wet. Probably from the snow. I push a little harder and he rolls to his side. I sit up. Spatters of red are covering the snow. Oh no. I pat down my body. Nothing hurts except my hip where it hit the ground. I check the Mayor. Blood is pouring out his shoulder. He's been shot. That's what the popping sound was. I hear a siren in the distance.

I take off my scarf and hold it to the wound. "Mayor Rollins, can you hear me?"

He groans again.

"Help is on the way. Just breathe. You're going to be fine." I hope so anyway.

The sirens are close. I hear a car door slam and glance up. Travis. Relief rushes through me. He hurries toward me as best he can in the deep snow. We got several inches the night before and it's really piling up.

"Autumn, are you okay? I heard the gun shots from the church." He scans me when he gets closer and his eyes land on the blood on my coat. They grow dark and his eyebrows pinch together forming a line between them.

"I'm fine, but the Mayor isn't." I glance down at the Mayor. His eyes are closed and his breathing is becoming shallower.

"What happened?" Travis bends down and checks the Mayor's pulse.

"We were talking and the next thing I know the Mayor pushes me to the ground and whoever was shooting at us got a few more rounds off before peeling out of here.

"Did you get a look at the vehicle?"

"Same dark SUV from the spa."

Travis frowns as two EMT's crouch beside us and begin to work on the Mayor. We step back and let them whisk the Mayor away.

I shiver in the cold although I don't feel cold. Maybe I'm in shock. Travis wraps an arm around my shoulder.

"Are you sure you're not hurt? Do you need to go to the hospital?"

I shake my head. "The Mayor saved me. I thought it was a car back firing." A tear falls from my eye, and I reach to brush it away when Travis catches my hand.

"Your hands are covered in blood." He uses his thumb and wipes away the tear. His touch sending a different kind of shiver down my spine. "Let's get you home and cleaned up. Then you can tell me what happened."

I nod and let him lead me toward his SUV, which is in the church parking lot. "What were you doing at the church?"

"I was actually at the school. Cat forgot her lunch in my car. When I went to drop it off they said she never showed up."

"Oh no! Did you call your house?"

He nods. "I did. She said she wasn't feeling well."

"Poor thing. She's been through a lot."

"She definitely has," he mutters.

When we reach his vehicle, he helps me in the passenger seat and buckles me up so I don't get blood on the seat. We wait for the ambulance to take off, sirens blaring with the Mayor tucked inside.

Travis grabs some hand wipes from the glove box and cleans my hands. "What were you doing out here?" He looks around. "Without your Jeep."

"Going for a walk."

He quirks an eyebrow. "In freezing temperatures?"

I shrug. "I needed some air."

He studies me. "Why are you walking out here?"

"It's away from my house."

"And you want to walk away from your house because..." he pauses. "I'm stumped. Am I missing something?"

I sigh and decide to tell him everything. "Me and Josh got in a fight. I didn't want to ride home with him so...that's why I'm walking out here."

"And you know he's out looking for you so you went the opposite way of your house."

"Pretty much."

He frowns. "What were you fighting about?"

I look out the window and bite my lip.

"Autumn?" He squeezes my arm. "Talk to me."

I glance down at his hand then into his eyes. "We were fighting about you."

"Me?"

"Josh thinks we're starting something again."

"And he doesn't like it." Travis clenches his jaw.

"No. He doesn't."

"Are we?"

"Are we what?"

"Starting something?"

I shrug.

"I never did explain things. What happened that night. Why I did what I did."

I close my eyes. Not ready to hear this, but needing to hear it.

"Autumn, I" Travis's scanner goes off.

"Suspect's vehicle heading South on Pine St."

Travis and I stare at each other for a moment before he turns on his siren and squeals onto the street.

16

"We lost them. How is that possible?" Travis paces back and forth in front of his SUV. Snow is falling around him and his yelling is making smoke come out his mouth like a fire breathing dragon. If he could breathe fire, I'm sure he would right now.

I cross my arms and snuggle into the heated leather seats in his SUV. One minute we're chasing the suspects down Pine street, they turn left then vanish.

Poof.

Gone.

No abandoned buildings to hide in.

Nothing but a few houses. All of them look empty this time of day. No lights on. No smoke coming from the chimney's. How could the SUV just disappear?

Travis is yelling again. His arm not holding the cellphone is waving around like a band conductor.

My phone buzzes in my pocket and I pull it out.

Josh.

I hit decline and tuck it away.

It rings again. I ignore it. The car falls silent for a moment then the ringing starts again.

I sigh and take it out.

It's Bethany.

"Hello?"

"Autumn, thank goodness." She sounds out of breath. "I was at the police station and just heard about the shooting. Are you alright?"

"I'm fine."

"And the Mayor?"

"He's at the hospital."

Silence.

"Bethany, are you there?"

Her voice comes out in a squeak. "Is he dead?"

"He was shot, but I'm optimistic. I'm going to have Travis drop me off there shortly."

"You're with Travis?"

I cringe. I shouldn't have mentioned that. Bethany thrived on gossip. Word would get around we were driving to the hospital together and the next thing you know, we're engaged and planning a June wedding. "He was the officer at the scene. I didn't have my car so he offered to give me a ride."

"Where's your Jeep?"

"At home."

"Why? Where's Josh?"

I sigh. "He's probably at his house."

"You mean you don't know." She sounds appalled.

"I'm not his keeper. Josh is free to go and do whatever he wants and so am I." I must have been talking loudly because Travis turns and cocks an eyebrow at me. I smile and wave. He turns back around and continues his conversation.

"I'm not trying to upset you. It's just. You and Josh. Everyone just assumes..." her voice trails off.

"Assumes what?"

"Nothing. It's silly."

"No, what? What does everyone assume?"

"Assumes you two are a couple. Dating. Secretly. We're all waiting for the official announcement and the wedding date."

"Our wedd-what?" I gasp. Actually, I start hyperventilating.

Travis chooses that moment to end his call and get in the car. He stares at me while I'm gasping into the phone, about ready to pass out from lack of air. My throat is closing in and I cough to get some air.

Bethany calls my name a couple of times. I find my voice and say, "I'll have to call you back." When I hang up, Travis pounces.

"Who was that? You look like someone told you Santa Claus was real."

"It's nothing." I tuck my phone away.

"Autumn. Please don't shut me out."

I shake my head, not ready to talk about it. "Silly town gossip," I mumble.

He nods and thankfully doesn't push the subject. "I need to go question the Mayor. He's out of surgery and should be able to talk soon. Do you want me to drop you off at your house or do you want to go to the hospital?"

Going home wasn't an option. I couldn't face Josh right now and know he'd be waiting for me. "The hospital. I want to thank the Mayor for saving me."

Travis stares ahead, but doesn't put the car in drive. "I saw you."

"Saw me what?" I turn to study his profile.

"You and Josh."

I scowl. "What?" I was in no mood to hear about me and Josh again.

"It was the night of the party. We were taking a break, but you smiled at me earlier in the day so I thought maybe you were ready to get back together. Maybe you finally decided to forgive me for drag racing those kids from Villsboro with you in the car."

I huff and mutter, "You almost killed us running that red light."

He rakes a hand through his hair. "I was a dumb teenager, what can I say. My ego got the best of me...still does sometimes," he smirks then continues, "I came over to apologize for the one hundredth time and see if you would go to dinner with me before the party. You were in a yellow sundress, swinging in your backyard swing. Your copper curls blowing in the wind. You were gorgeous." His eyes are staring straight ahead as if he's lost in the memory. He gulps then continues, "Josh was pushing you. You were laughing and looking back at him. You never looked at me like that."

I frown. "Like what?"

"So, carefree. So, in...so in love."

I almost throw up in my mouth. "I've never—,"

He cuts me off, "You were laughing so hard at something he said you fell out of the swing. I dropped the sunflowers I bought for you and started to rush toward you, but he caught you then he...he kissed you." Travis turns to me. Tears are in his eyes.

My eyes grow wide. "On the forehead."

Travis closes his eyes and turns away from me. "You don't have to lie about it, Autumn. I know what I saw."

I narrow my eyes at him. "What exactly did you see?"

He caught you in his arms and held you close to his chest. I saw him drop his head to yours.

I snort. "He was telling me how clumsy I am."

Travis shakes his head and frowns. "I saw— I mean I'm pretty sure."

I cross my arms and raise an eyebrow. "You saw my best friend catch me after I fell out of the swing because I am that klutzy. He made fun of me and kissed my forehead. End of story. I had dinner with my parents then waited like an idiot for you to come pick me up. When you never showed, I assumed you weren't ready to get back together. The next morning, I woke up to the news of you and April..." I can't bring myself to say it. I feel like I'm going to be sick. I need air. I push open the car door and step into the cold.

"Autumn, wait." Travis scrambles around the car and tries to pull me into his arms.

I shrug him off and demand, "Why didn't you say anything? In the yard, why didn't you call out to me? Demand to know what was going on?"

Travis hangs his head. "It gutted me. I felt numb. Josh was...is your shadow. He's always there. You told me you two were a package deal. Assured me you were just friends." He runs a hand through his red hair again.

I shake my head. "So, you hooked up with April because you thought I wanted to be with Josh?"

"No. I was angry. Started drinking at the party, too much. April offered to drive me home. She was sympathetic. Nice. Understanding. One thing led to another...I woke up with a huge hangover and little re-collection of the night before. When I started sobering up and I began piecing things together..." he didn't need to finish, I knew the story.

I open my mouth, but have no idea what to say. A silly

misunderstanding led to years of pain, even a baby. It's like a soap opera. The whole thing makes me sad.

"I'm sorry, Autumn." Travis takes my hand. "I should have handled things differently. Should have talked to you then we would have gotten back together. Graduated and gone off to college together, maybe even have gotten married. Cat would be our daughter."

I try to swallow the lump forming in my throat. We could have had a life together. Maybe be raising a family together. I gasp for air as a cry escapes my mouth and I reach up to try and smother it.

Travis wraps his arms around me as I sob into his chest. He strokes my hair and tries to soothe me. I feel heartbroken all over again although I'm not sure my heart has ever healed. "I'm so sorry, Autumn."

"Me too."

His cell phone goes off. He ignores it, but it rings again. "I better get that."

I nod into his chest as he reluctantly lets me go, but he keeps ahold of my hand when he answers.

"Cat, slow down. What's wrong?"

I perk up at the mention of Cat's name. All I can hear is sobbing on the other end of the line. My heart seems to ache even more. At this rate, it'll never heal.

"I'm on my way." He hangs up and pulls me toward his car.

"What's wrong?"

"I have no idea. She's just sobbing into the phone."

I slide into the passenger seat as he shuts the door and hurries around to the driver's side.

He hesitates for a moment and turns to me. "Autumn, I want you to know...I've never stopped loving you."

I want to tell him I feel the same way, but I'm not sure I do. I need time to think. I simply nod and say, "Cat needs you right now."

He flips on the siren and for the second time while I'm in his car, he runs every red light in town.

17

I stare at Travis's house. It's a three-bedroom white ranch style home with a large front porch. It's quaint, it definitely suits him. Even has a white picket fence around the front yard.

Travis is out of the car and racing up the stone side walk.

I hesitate. Going into Travis's home seems intimate, even strange. I'm not sure I'm ready for this then I mentally scold myself for being silly. Cat is upset. I need to be there for her. I push open my door and hurry up the sidewalk after Travis.

We barely make it to the porch when Cat comes running outside. We both freeze.

Travis's mouth hangs open.

I blink and try to process what I'm seeing.

Cat is standing on the porch in blue and white flannel pajamas. Tears are streaming down her face and for good reason.

Her once red hair is now white like really white. It matches the snow piling up in her lawn. Her pale skin and white hair almost run together.

No one says anything, we just stare at her head.

"It's so white. The bottle didn't say it would turn my hair white. I only wanted to add a few blond highlights." She glances at me, her eyes brimming with tears.

Travis appears to be in shock.

I step forward and take Cat's hand. "I think we should call your aunt."

She nods. Her lower lip quivering. "I fell asleep. Left it in too long. When I woke up it was like this."

I wrap an arm around her shoulder and whisper in her ear, "We've all been here." I shoot Travis a look and he finally snaps out of his trance.

"It's not so bad," he offers.

Cat scowls and starts to cry.

I give him a dirty look and he cringes. "In high school, I wanted to have blond hair, remember Travis?"

His face lights up and he starts to chuckle. I love the sound of it. It's low and deep. Another shiver goes up my spine. Get it together, Autumn.

"It was awful. Much worse than yours." He cringes again when he sees Cat's eyes grow wide and tears fall down her face again. "I mean yours isn't awful. It's really not that bad." Travis runs a hand through his hair.

I shake my head and smirk. "Ignore him. He stuck his foot in his mouth in high school too. I didn't speak to him for a week."

Cat smiles and wipes her tears.

I squeeze her shoulder. "Your Aunt Regina was a miracle worker. My hair was back to normal in no time and I finally spoke to your father again."

"Only after I sent you sunflowers and chocolate," Travis grumbles, following us inside.

"And kept showing up on my doorstep, like a lost puppy." I sit down on the leather couch.

Cat laughs and curls up next to me. "Do you think Aunt Regina can really fix this?"

"Absolutely. If anyone can, it's your aunt." I look up at Travis.

He's watching us with a strange expression on his face. I cock my head and raise my eyebrows. He snaps out of it and fumbles for his phone. "I'll call her right now. The shop doesn't close until six, but I'm sure she'll make an exception plus..." He peeks outside. "The snow is really coming down. Temperatures are dropping. She'll need to close up early to make it home safely." He steps from the room and makes the call.

My cell phone buzzes in my pocket, but I ignore it. I glance around the room and take in the masculine feel. Beige walls, Leather couches and chairs, dark wood furniture, flat screen on the wall above the fireplace, it was all very Travis. My phone buzzes again.

"Are you going to get that?" Cat moves over so I can get my phone.

I sigh. I know who it is, but pull it out anyway. Josh. I hover over the decline button, but know he'll call again especially since it's after four and the sun is starting to set.

"Hello."

"Autumn, thank God. I've been worried sick. Where are you? I heard about the shooting. Are you at the hospital? I'll be there in a few minutes." He's nervous. Josh always rambles when he's nervous or worried.

A part of me feels bad. I should have called him after the shooting, but I'm still not ready to talk to him. "I'm at..." I pause. He'll flip out if he knows I'm at Travis's. "At a friend's." I glance over at Cat. She's pretending not to listen and is studying her white painted finger nails. "She's having a bit of a crisis so I'm helping her out."

Cat looks up at me and grins.

I wink at her.

"Oh." Silence. "I can come get you when you're done."

"I'm fine. I'll get a ride."

"Look Autumn."

I cut him off. "I can't talk right now, Josh."

Travis enters the room and stops short when I say Josh's name. Our eyes lock. He shakes his head and heads back into the kitchen.

"When will you be home?" Josh's question snaps me from my trance.

"I'm not sure. I really have to go." I hang up before he can say anything else.

"Was that your boyfriend?" Cat asks me. Her voice barely a whisper.

"No, my best friend."

Cat nods. "So, you're single?"

I sigh. "Yep."

"My dad is too."

I shift on the couch. Is Cat trying to play matchmaker?

Travis clears his throat.

My face flushes as I meet his eyes. He winks at me and I can feel it grow hotter if it's even possible.

Cat giggles. "You still like my dad, don't you?"

I open my mouth to protest, but Travis cuts me off. "Aunt Regina should be here any second. She closed the shop early due to the snow and is on her way home." He moves toward Cat and wraps an arm around her shoulder. "Why did you dye your hair, honey?"

Cat's expression turns serious and she drops her eyes to her hands then sniffles. "I wanted to look more like mom."

Travis frowns and glances at me. His eyes filled with questions, but I can tell he's scared to ask them.

I'm at a loss for what to say. I get it, but have no clue how to handle this. "Cat, your hair is beautiful. Your mom loved your hair."

"She did?" Cat stares up at me. Her green eyes wide and filled with tears.

I reach out and push her white hair behind her shoulder. "She was always talking about how pretty your hair was and wished she had hair like yours."

Cat shook her head. "She was always complaining about it. Saying I looked too much like my dad."

I wipe a tear away from her cheek. "That's not a bad thing." I refuse to meet Travis's eyes. I can feel them on me, but I know if I look, I'll be a goner.

"Dad is pretty cute, isn't he?" Cat sniffles and looks at me expectantly.

I nod. "Very."

Cat smiles and then wraps her arms around me.

I return the hug and stroke her hair, which smells like ammonia. When she lets go and sits back, I say, "Don't ever think you need to look or be like anyone else. You're perfect just the way you are."

She blushes and whispers, "Thank you."

A rush of cold air fills the room as Regina bursts through the front door. "Oh Lordy, it's colder than the Arctic tundra out there." She stomps her boots on the Home Sweet Home mat and brushes the snow off her red hair then stops short when she sees Cat. "What did you do?" She rushes over and starts running her finger through Cat's fried hair.

Cat bursts into tears and Regina consoles her while ushering her to the bathroom, completely ignoring us.

Silence fills the living room. Travis looks over at me. "So, you think I'm 'very cute'?"

I roll my eyes.

He chuckles. "Are you hungry?"

My stomach growls in response.

"I'll take that as a 'yes'. What sounds good?"

Before I can answer his cell phone rings.

"Hold that thought." He holds up his index finger while he answers the phone. "Detective Mills." He murmurs a few things into the phone then hangs up. "We've got to go."

"Where?"

"The hospital. The Mayor's awake. He's asking for you."

"Me? Why me?" I stand and slip on my jacket.

Travis shrugs. "Let's go find out."

18

I shiver as I enter the hospital. The waiting room is practically empty except for Bobby. He's dressed in a dark suit. His head is in his hands and he's staring at the floor.

Travis walks to the desk to inquire about the Mayor so I make a beeline for Bobby.

"Bobby?" I place a hand on his shoulder and he jumps. "Sorry."

His stares up at me with a blank look in his eyes. Dark circles are underneath his eyes and his hair is sticking up in all directions as if he keeps running a hand through it. "Autumn, what are you doing here?"

"The Mayor asked to see me."

"He did? Why?"

I shrug. "No clue. What are you doing here?"

"The Mayor. He's the only family I have left." He stares at his hands. I forgot his parents died a few years ago. His dad had a heart attack in his hardware store and his mom passed away in her sleep a year later.

I sit down next to Bobby and bite my lip. I'm not sure if

this is the right time to bring up the case, but I'm on a time crunch and the bodies are piling up. "Did you ever find anything on the Mayor? Anything April had on him?"

Bobby shakes his head. "I searched her records. Her office. Our bedroom. Nothing. I'm thinking of hiring a private investigator. Someone has got it in for the Mayor. I think April was killed because she found out about something. Something the Mayor was into."

"Like what?"

He shrugs. "I don't know. Hence the private investigator."

I frown. "So, you think April and Vicky's murders aren't related?"

He makes a face. "Why would they be? They didn't run in the same circles. It seems like we'd be grasping at straws to link them."

I open my mouth to object when I hear my name. "Autumn. The Mayor will see us now."

Bobby looks back and forth between me and Travis. "You two are talking?" When we don't respond, he huffs and mutters. "Guess something good came from April's death."

I'm not sure how to respond so I pat his knee and get up. Travis has a blank look on his face as if he's not sure what to make of Bobby's comment. April wasn't keeping us from talking...was she?

I follow Travis down the hallway as a million questions keep running through my mind. I push them aside and focus on what I'm going to ask the Mayor. When we get to the end of the hall, Travis stops and looks around. "That's strange."

"What?"

"Officer Dane is supposed to be guarding the Mayor."

I look up and down the hall and don't see anyone. "Maybe he went to get some coffee."

Travis shakes his head. "Not without another officer relieving him. Someone tried to kill the Mayor. The Captain ordered 24/7 protection. Somethings not right." He pushes open the door to the Mayor's room and stops short.

I bump into him and raise an eyebrow. "Travis." When he doesn't move or respond, my heart starts beating like a stampede in my chest. "What's wrong?"

"The Mayor."

"What about him?" I try to peek over his shoulder, but he's too tall.

"He's gone."

"Gone?" I step around him to find an empty hospital bed. "Maybe they took him to X-ray or to run more tests."

Travis shakes his head. "The nurse said he was in his room...resting."

"Maybe she was wrong. I'll go ask." I turn to leave.

Travis reaches out and squeezes my shoulder. "No, I'll go. I need to find Officer Dane and call the Captain. You stay here in case the Mayor comes back."

I watch him walk to the nurses' station then turn back to the empty room. I shiver. This is the same room Vicky was killed in. Maybe it's cursed. I shake the thoughts from my head and think about the Mayor. Where could he be? Surely, he didn't just get up and walk out of the hospital. He was shot. Just had surgery. Leaving would be hazardous to his health.

His bed is disheveled. The pillows are practically hanging off the bed as though someone knocked them off. A blue blanket and the sheet are pulled to one side and a cell phone is tucked underneath it. I glance toward the door and see Travis talking to a nurse. The silver phone is shining back at me. It won't hurt to take a peek.

I pick up the phone and press the button on the side. A

text flashes across the screen. It's from a private number. It reads. *Meet at the drop off spot with $50,000 or else I go public.* A noise from the hall makes me tuck the phone back in the bed. Travis enters the room with a young petite blond nurse, named Hallie.

Her brown eyes grow wide as she takes in the empty room. "He was here ten minutes ago."

Travis rubs his eyes. "He couldn't just get up and walk out of here, right?"

The nurse shakes her head. "He would have to pass the nurse's station, unless..."

"Unless what?" Travis snaps then cringes. "Sorry."

The nurse nods and then gestures toward the fire door across from the room. "Unless he went through there. The alarm is broken so anyone can enter or leave without being noticed. Although he was in no condition to leave." She shifts back and forth. "I've got to talk to my supervisor and let her know what's going on."

"Call if you hear anything." Travis hands her a business card before she hurries back down the hall. He stares at the empty bed. His eyebrows are pinched together and appears to be deep in thought.

I open my mouth to point out the phone, but a groan comes from the behind the fire door.

Travis reaches for his gun and puts a finger to his lips. He creeps toward the fire door as I watch from the Mayor's room. My palms begin to sweat and my heart pounds in my chest. It's so loud, I'm sure Travis can hear it. He sneaks a peek at me before pushing open the door.

"Officer Dane?"

I let out the breath I'm holding and move toward the fire door. Travis's bends down next to Officer Dane. Officer Dane is the same age as we are, but years on the force have not been good to him. His dark hair is already speckled with gray and a few wrinkles line his forehead, which also sports a huge bump on it. "What happened?" Travis asks, helping up his fellow officer.

"I'm not sure." Officer Dane replies, rubbing his head. "One minute I was checking on the Mayor and the next I'm waking up with a splitting headache."

I crouch down and assess his wound. "You don't remember getting hit?"

Officer Dane shakes his head.

I'm not sure I believe him, but head wounds are fickle. "We better have a doctor look at you."

Travis holds on to Officer Dane's arm as they make their way down the hallway. I trail behind them thinking about the day. The photo I found earlier flashes through my mind. I need to go back to the spa and check out the file. I feel like it's the key to this puzzle.

"Autumn?"

I look up to see Josh standing in the waiting room. Travis and Officer Dane have disappeared. I must have zoned out. "How did you know I was here?"

"Bobby called me."

I glance around the waiting room and as if Josh can read my mind he says, "He left. Something about needing to get some answers."

"Answers?"

Josh shrugs. "He didn't elaborate and I didn't push."

"Did he say where he was going?"

"No, why?"

"The Mayor is missing."

"Missing?"

I nod.

Josh frowns. "You think Bobby had something to do with it?"

I shrug.

"I walked him out. He was alone. There's no way he could have gotten the Mayor out of here."

"Unless he had help."

"Autumn." Josh rakes a hand through his wet hair. He's still wearing his leather bomber jacket. His dark jeans have a little bit of snow on the cuff and his boots are still covered with snow. Obviously, he hasn't been here long, which didn't give Bobby and whoever he is working with a lot of time to get the Mayor out of here without Josh seeing them.

"You're sure he left alone?"

"Autumn, Bobby drove off as I came back inside. There's no way he 'kidnapped' the Mayor."

"Maybe he pretended to drive off, but really drove around the side of the building and picked up whoever took the Mayor."

"And who took the Mayor?" Josh crosses his arms over his chest and raises an eyebrow.

I bite my lip. My mind was going a million miles an hour and I'm grasping at straws. This whole case doesn't make sense. If Vicky killed April because April was going to start a new spa in town then who killed Vicky and why? The Mayor was shot, is now missing and looks like he is being blackmailed. The Mayor was the key, I know it, but how?

"We need to go to the spa."

19

I take a sip of Chamomile tea and stew. Josh didn't take me to the spa, he took me home. I'm sitting in my favorite MU sweatshirt and black yoga pants snuggled up on the couch. Josh fed me beef stew and shoved my favorite tea mug in my hand.

He insisted we get home before the weather got any worse. We did slide into the driveway so I guess he has a point. I sigh. The snow is really hindering my ability to look into this case. Not to mention I'm still mad at my BFF. A subject we are both tiptoeing around.

Josh hates confrontation and I can't say I love it, but we need to discuss things. After everything Travis told me, I need time to process my feelings and figure out how to move forward.

My phone rings interrupting my thoughts. Travis's name flashes across it. I should pick it up. Josh and I left the hospital quickly. I gave one of the nurses a message telling him I'd left, but it still wasn't the same as actually saying 'good-bye'.

Josh snorts when he sees who's calling, but doesn't say

anything.

I ignore him and tap a finger on the rim of my cup as I stare into the fire.

"Autumn...I'm sorry."

I tear my gaze from the fire and lock eyes with my best friend. I hate fighting with him, but I also refuse to be in the middle of some weird triangle. "I know," I whisper and take a sip of tea.

"Please talk to me."

I shake my head. "I can't right now. The Mayor is missing. Someone is stalking me. Shooting at me. I need to solve this case then figure out the rest of my life."

Josh nods. "What can I do to help?"

There's my BFF. "Where's the file folder from Cat?"

"I think it's still in the Jeep."

"Can you get it?"

He gets up and shrugs on his coat. "Do you think there's something in there that will help you solve this case?"

"I sure hope so because I'm coming up empty."

Josh opens the front door and lets in a blast of cold air. I hunker down and snuggle into the white chenille blanket on my blue plushy couch. He's back in a few minutes with a file folder in his hand. He hands it to me then goes back to check the lock and peek out the front window.

"What's wrong?"

"Maybe nothing. I felt like I was being watched."

I sit up and push the blinds apart to stare out onto the empty street. Snow is still coming down and the yard is covered in a blanket of snow. Only a few houses still have lights on; it is after ten o'clock on a Monday night. The street's empty, but I also get the feeling we're being watched. I close the binds and move onto the floor so I can spread the file out on the coffee table. It's not as thick as I remember it. Weren't there more papers? I open it and gasp.

"What is it?"

"Nothing."

Josh furrows his brows. "What do you mean nothing?"

I hold up the white pieces of paper. "Nothing but blank sheets of paper."

"What?!"

"Someone must have broken into the Jeep. I really should start locking it. What is this town coming too? Murder, kidnapping, break-ins."

Josh wipes a hand over his face and sits down next to me. "I don't like this, Autumn. Maybe you should let the police handle this."

I can smell the tea tree and mint on his sweater. It usually comforts me, but I don't feel very calm. Someone is trying very hard to make sure I don't piece all this together. I'm not sure what to think.

"Autumn?"

"We need to write down what we know. So much has happened and I need to get it all straight in my mind."

Josh grumbles something I can't make out. I can feel his eyes on me as I get up and retrieve a notebook and pen from the book shelf. I'm a note taker. A visual person. I need to see what we're working with. I flip open the book and write out April's name then circle it, make a line and add Vicky's name along with her motive, 'rival spa'. I make another line from April's name to the Mayor then write 'blackmail and broke'. I bite the end of the pen and stare at the paper.

"What about Sally and the good Dr.?"

"Cat did say Sally and Vicky were talking in the office when she went to use the restroom. It's possible they were working together, but why? Sally has only been in town for a month."

"Maybe they bonded over their hatred for April?"

I frown. "Do you think Sally told Vicky about coming to town to get her boyfriend back? It seems like something you would share with a friend not your employer."

"True, but Sally doesn't know a lot of people. Vicky gave her job." Josh shrugs.

Something didn't feel right. Then I remember the photo. "Josh, I found something...in Vicky's office."

"What?"

"A photo."

"A photo of what?"

"The Mayor and...Vicky."

"So."

"They were kissing."

Josh's mouth drops open. "Vicky and the Mayor? Are you sure?"

I nod. "They were young though. Maybe our age."

"That was over twenty year ago. The Mayor was still married."

"I know." I rub my temples. A headache's starting to form.

"You don't think..."

"What?"

"Bethany's father was overseas in the Army, right?"

"So."

"Maybe he's not Bethany's father."

My jaw drops. "Bethany does favor her mother, but I remember Bethany's dad. She has his nose and some of his mannerisms. The Mayor and Vicky may have had an affair, but I don't think Bethany was a product of it."

Josh shrugs. "It's just a theory."

I bite my lip and try to remember back twenty years ago. I was only thirteen. Adult drama wasn't something I was into, but I do remember babysitting for Vicky several nights a week after Bethany was born. She worked late at the spa trying to make ends meet. Her husband was killed in a military raid shortly after Bethany was born. Maybe Vicky got lonely. Turned to the Mayor for comfort. Josh clears his throat and pulls me from my thoughts.

"Autumn?"

"Hmm?"

"Are you with me?"

"Of course. I was just thinking about your theory. I still don't believe Bethany is the Mayor's daughter. Vicky was madly in love with her husband. She was crushed when he died."

"I know. She still has a photo of him in her office." Josh hangs his head as if he feels guilty for even thinking she would cheat on her husband. "Where did you find the photo of Vicky and the Mayor?"

"In a secret compartment in the desk. There was a file too, but I didn't get a chance to look at it. We need to get to the spa and see what's in there before someone else finds it."

"Do you think the person trying to break into the spa was looking for that file?"

"Possibly...I don't know. None of this makes any sense." My phone rings again. Travis's name pops up again.

Josh scowls. "I'll get some more tea. You better answer or he'll keep calling." He snags my cup and stomps into the kitchen.

I sigh and pick up the call before it goes to voicemail. "Hello."

"Autumn, are you ok?"

"Yes, why?"

"You left the hospital without a word. A nurse told me you left with a man."

"Josh came to pick me up. I wasn't sure when you would be able to leave so I came home."

"Oh." He sounds disappointed.

"Did you find the Mayor?"

"Not yet."

"What about Officer Dane? Does he remember anything?"

"Autumn," Travis growls. "You know I can't discuss this with you."

"Fine." I snap. Silence fills the airways then I sigh and ask, "How's Cat? Did Regina fix her hair?"

"I just got off the phone with her. She's officially a red head again."

I smile. "That's good. Red heads are cuter than blonds."

"Are they now?" I can hear the smile in his voice.

"I've always been a fan."

"Good to hear." Someone said something to him. "Autumn, I've got to go."

"Is everything ok?"

"We have a lead on the Mayor?"

"Let me know when you find him." I want to add I hope he's alive, but I keep the thought to myself. "Be careful, Travis."

"I will. Call you later?"

"Please."

"Bye, Autumn."

"Bye, Travis." I hang up and stare at the phone. A sinking feeling forms in the pit of my stomach. Is this how cop's girlfriends and wives feel when they get off the phone with their loved ones? If so, I'm not sure dating Travis is such a good idea. Visions of awful things happening to him flash through my mind.

"Did he find the Mayor?"

I jump and drop the pen I'm holding. "Um, no."

"Sorry, didn't mean to scare you." Josh sets my tea mug next to me. "Everything ok? Did Travis accuse you of kidnapping the Mayor? You're as white as the blanket." He gestures to the blanket on my lap.

"No, how could I kidnap the Mayor? I was with Travis the whole time..." I pause and watch my best friend's face fall. I hadn't meant to let that slip. I decide to change the subject. "Back to our suspect list." I add in Sally and Dr. Gregory with question marks by their name and write affair under Dr. Gregory's name and jealous girlfriend by Sally's name. "Their whole situation confuses me too. I know April was manipulative. Travis and Cat are proof and so is Bobby, but why bring Dr. Gregory here? Why not fly to Chicago to get treatments? She certainly had the money, what was the benefit of bringing him to Daysville?"

"He's a specialist. Maybe his treatments required more visits and it was easier to bring him here then fly there."

"I guess, but it still doesn't feel right. Why didn't Bobby go to any of these appointments?"

"I don't know. Maybe he did. You could ask him."

"Good idea." I pick up my phone and pause.

"What?"

"You don't think Bobby is involved with any of this, do you?"

"Both he and Nikki had every reason to kill April, but I don't think they did and they had no reason to kill Vicky. Didn't we rule them out?"

"Bobby wasn't at the spa unless he was the one trying to

break-in, but Cat would have seen him, right? It's not like it's easy for him to hide."

"Unless he and Cat…" Josh trails off.

I pursue my lips. "Cat didn't kill her mother." I pause and think about the facts. "I don't think Bobby or Nikki did either. They're not going on the list. I think I have this narrowed down, but I don't have enough to go on yet." I scroll through my phone and tap Bobby's number.

His phone rings and then goes to voicemail. I leave a message telling him to call me and hang up.

"It is kind of late. He's probably asleep."

I nod and study my suspect list again. I draw a circle around Vicky and begin to draw lines to the suspects who could have killed her. I was having a hard time coming up with any. "Sally and Dr. Gregory were both at the hospital, but Sally told us she was talking to Dr. Gregory and didn't learn of Vicky's death until Bethany told her about it. Dr. Gregory was at the hospital, but was with Sally since she was trying to convince him to move back to Chicago."

"So, they're each other's alibis, that's convenient," Josh mutters.

"Right?" I draw a line from Sally and Dr. Gregory to Vicky. "What's their motive?"

"Motive?"

"Why kill Vicky? They're leaving town. What's the benefit?" If she killed April or was taking the fall for April's death based on Cat's testimony, why kill her?"

"Tying up loose ends. Making sure she doesn't incriminate them?"

"Maybe. It still doesn't make sense why they were working together. What's the connection? I feel like we're missing something."

Josh yawns.

I glance at the clock. It's pushing eleven. "Let's stick a pin in this and get some sleep."

"I'll take the couch." He plops down and covers up with a blanket before I can protest.

"You could take the guest room," I mutter to myself because he's already asleep.

His eyes are closed and soft snores escape his lips.

I roll my eyes and turn toward my bedroom when I hear a soft knock on the front door. It's late. Who could be knocking?

20

I'm a little more than nervous to answer the door especially with someone stalking and shooting at me. I could ignore it, but the sleuth in me really wants to solve this case. I peek through the peep hole and let out the breath I'm holding. I flip the lock and open the door. "Bobby, what are you doing here?"

"I got your message." He holds up his phone.

"I just left it." I frown. "You could have just called me back." I gesture for him to come in and shut the door and lock it.

"I was already on my way over to see you. The roads are a little dicey so I didn't want to risk talking and driving."

Josh stirs on the couch, but doesn't wake up. So much for my strong and protective body guard.

"Let's go in the kitchen so we don't wake him," I whisper and motion for him to follow me. "Do you want something to drink? Water? Tea?"

"I'm good. Thanks."

I gesture to the wooden chairs. "Have a seat."

He sits down and places a file folder on the table. "To

answer your question, I only went to a handful of April's appointments. She struggled with endometriosis. Suffered several miscarriages. Supposedly, Dr. Gregory was a specialist in the field although I never felt like he really knew anything more than any other doctor we saw through the years." He looks down at the folder in his hands. "Guess it doesn't matter, now."

I reach out and squeeze his hand. "I'm sorry, Bobby."

He shakes his head. "It's probably best we never had a child together. Maybe a blessing in its own way. We weren't really in love and having a child would have made things more...difficult." He gulps and blinks back tears before shaking his head again. "Anyway, I think I found something."

"What is it?" I'm anxious to see what he has, but a part of me feels bad for not letting Travis in on everything I know so far. "Did you call Travis?"

Bobby quirks an eyebrow. "Why would I call Travis?"

"Because he's the detective on your wife's murder investigation."

"Travis blows me off all the time. I think he resents me for getting to spend so much time with Cat when she was growing up. I can't help it the man chose to be a cop and works crazy hours." He shrugs his shoulders then gets down to business. "This may be nothing, but I think it's important and I know you won't ignore me especially since it sounds like someone is after you now." Bobby's leg was bouncing up and down.

I gulp. The man has a point. "Whatcha got?"

Bobby slides the folder over to me. "I found this in April's SUV. The police didn't search it since it technically wasn't part of the crime scene. I've been so busy with the funeral arrangements and tying up loose ends I just got around to picking it up from the spa today. This slid out from underneath the seat."

I pick up the folder and open it. There are several photos of the Mayor and Vicky. One is of them kissing, but it's recent. Vicky's hair was shorter and curlier and the Mayor is gray. "So, the Mayor and Vicky were still seeing each other."

"Still? What are you talking about?" Bobby frowns.

Shoot, I hadn't meant to let that piece of information slip. "I found a photo of the Mayor and Vicky kissing about twenty years ago."

"Twenty years ago?! He was still married to April's mom."

I nod.

"So, the Mayor was having an affair. I knew it."

"You did?"

"In middle school, I saw them together one evening in the park. It was after football practice. I was supposed to meet my mom at the café and I was late. I took a shortcut through the park and saw them sitting on a park bench together. Vicky was crying and the Mayor was holding her. I figured he was simply being a friend, comforting a widow, but as I look back on it, it seemed like it was something more. They both looked sad as if they were grieving something together."

"Grieving together? What could they be grieving? The Mayor wasn't a friend of Vicky's husband, was he?"

Bobby shakes his head. "No, I don't recall the Mayor ever having any friends."

"Ever? That's sad."

"The man is money hungry. It's all he cares about. Money and his reputation."

"Hmm."

"What?"

"I just wonder if there was something else they shared."

"Like what?"

"A child?"

Bobby laughs. "April was the Mayor's only child. I mean Bethany looks just like her mom, but I can see some of her dad in her. There's no way she's the Mayor's daughter."

I stare down at the recent photo of Vicky and the Mayor. "I guess you're right, but what's with the photos? The blackmail? Why wouldn't Vicky and the Mayor just come out in the open, say they were dating. Why the secrecy? Both of their spouses are dead. Their children are grown. It doesn't make sense."

"April would have thrown a fit if she found out the Mayor was dating Vicky. Those two never got along."

"Why?" My headache's pounding behind my eyes, but I need more details. I have to push on.

"Some ridiculous feud between April's mom and Vicky. I can't remember what it was about." He frowns and rubs a hand over his scruffy face.

"A feud…do you think April's mom knew about the affair?"

"Probably. She knew about everything; sometimes it seemed like she had the gossip even before it happened."

I snort. "Or created it."

"True," Bobby scoffs.

I study the photos again. "Looks like the park was their meeting place, which is odd, it's usually busy."

"Not where this bench is located. It's on the back side of the pond, kind of tucked back in the trees. A great place for privacy, if you know what I mean." He wiggles his eyebrows up and down.

I laugh because his bushy eyebrows wiggling up and down look ridiculous then cover my mouth so not to wake up Josh. "What do you think these photos have to do with April and Vicky's murders."

"Cat heard Vicky kill April. Maybe April was blackmailing her."

I raise my eyebrows at him. "How do you know about Cat's testimony?

He gives me a look. "Small town, Autumn. Everyone knows about what Cat heard at the spa the day April died."

"Right. I keep forgetting this town's gossip mill churns 24/7."

Bobby smirks. "Gotta love a small town."

"I guess." I bite my lip. "Small town gossip isn't helping us catch a killer though. Surely, someone knows something."

Bobby shrugs. "What if the Mayor killed Vicky?"

"Because he found out she killed April?"

Bobby nods.

"It's possible, but who is trying to break into the spa and why? And who shot the Mayor? He has to be working with someone or someone has it out for him."

Bobby frowns. "I hadn't thought of that. Maybe the Mayor owes someone money."

The text on his phone comes to mind, but I don't share it with Bobby.

"Hmm. Then I've got nothing."

I pat his hand. "We'll figure this out. Thanks for bring these by. Can I keep them?"

"They're all yours." Bobby yawns and moves to stand up then sits down. "Autumn, please find out who killed April. I know she was an awful person most of the time, but I saw glimpses of her no one else did. I grew to love her in my own way. She didn't deserve to die. Not like she did. Please, I'm not going to be able to move on until I get her justice."

"I know how you feel. She was once my best friend. I loved her before she stole Travis. Then I hated her, but you're right, she didn't deserve to die like that. I promise you, we'll find out who killed her and Vicky and hopefully we'll find the Mayor...alive."

"What do you mean?"

"Didn't you hear the Mayor is missing?"

"No." Bobby jumps up. His face goes pale as he starts to pace the kitchen. "I thought he was still in the hospital. When did this happen?"

"Right after I left you in the waiting room. The officer watching him was knocked out. Someone kidnapped him... or he left on his own accord, which I doubt."

Bobby groans. "I knew I should have hired personal security for him." He sits back down. "There's something else. I didn't want to tell anyone this, but April was getting strange messages on her cell phone. She only had one message saved from the day before she died, but the phone records show a call every day for the past two weeks from a blocked number."

"What kind of strange messages?"

"Someone telling April to meet them at the park with another $5,000 if she wants more information. I checked our bank statements and April withdrew $5,000 of cash every day for two weeks."

"Sally." I slap my hand over my mouth, I hadn't meant for her name to slip out. I need to gain a filter if I'm going to be successful at this sleuthing business.

"Sally? What does Sally have to do with this?"

I sigh. No use trying to back track now especially if Sally's story is starting to have cracks in it. "Sally told me she was blackmailing April. Found out a bunch of stuff about her and I guess me."

"What did she find?"

"I don't know. Sally gave me the folder, but I left it in the Jeep and someone stole it. They left me a bunch of blank papers. I guess I'm getting close to figuring this all out, but I feel like I'm not."

Bobby places a hand over mind. "Autumn, you need to be careful. I know I asked you to look into this, but I would never forgive myself if something happened to you not to mention Nikki would kill me."

I smile and pat his hand. "I'll be fine. My body guard is primed and ready to protect me."

"Body guard?" Bobby cocks his head to the side.

I stand and move into the living room. "He's quite a force to be reckon with." I stifle a laugh as Josh snorts in his sleep and drool drips onto the couch cushion.

"I bet he is." He pats my shoulder. "Just promise me you'll be careful."

"I will." I walk him to the door and wave to him as he leaves before locking the front door. Bobby's concerned words are running through my mind, but I can't stop. Not until this case is solved.

21

It's Thursday. A week since I've been here and for the same reason. A funeral. Only this time it's not April's, it's Vicky's. I'm seated in between Bethany and Josh with my back against the cold wooden pew. My black dress is freshly dry cleaned and pressed although I must say I hadn't planned on wearing it again for a long time. I'm fidgeting with the funeral program, which outlines Vicky's life. Her smiling photo is staring back at me with the phrases such as loving wife, mother, respected business owner, and upstanding member of the community written below it.

I glance up at Preacher John as he reads another scripture. A fleck of saliva lands on my program. I never sit in the first row for this very reason, but Bethany asked and I couldn't deny her. She's sniffling next to me in a black pant suit, her hair braided to one side. Her nose is bright red, eyes puffy and mascara's running down her cheeks. I place an arm around her and give her a gentle squeeze. The poor girl has no one left. Both of her parents are dead. So are her grandparents. Vicky was an only child so there are no aunts or uncles or even cousins to comfort her. My heart aches for her.

Another speck of saliva flies across the pulpit. Josh's pants are unfortunately the landing spot. He's looking dapper in his black suit and striped tie. His hair is kind of messy, but the beachy look works for him. Miss Violet Viles keeps sneaking glances his way. She's sitting a couple rows back and I can feel her eyes on us. Josh is of course oblivious to any of this. I've nudged him a few times and nodded her way, but he seems intent on paying attention to Preacher John. I probably should be too, but as I've mentioned before, I hate funerals. My skin is crawling and I'm ready to get out of this dress asap.

Not to mention, the Mayor is still missing. Mother Nature put a crimp in searching for him when she decided to dump close to three more inches of snow on us and the freezing temps weren't making it easy for crews to clear the roads so everyone was pretty much snow bound. Travis did call yesterday, but he didn't have any updates, at least none he cared to share with me. The tip they got turned out to be a bust. A few high schoolers had tied up one of the boy's little brothers and had put him in the trunk to scare him. Ms. Harriet lives across the street and thought it was the Mayor they were stuffing in the trunk. The little brother was fine, but the parents were livid. I can't say I blame them. So, there are currently no leads on the Mayor's whereabouts.

Travis did offer to escort me to the funeral, but I came early to support Bethany. Me and Josh are still tiptoeing around each other. Our conversations are short and stiff. I miss my best friend, but I'm not sure how to find common ground with him or Travis. I've decided I need some time.

Time to think, clear my head, focus on solving this case then I can figure out what to do with these boys. Yes, boys because that's how they're acting.

More saliva lands on my program and I sigh. I'm definitely taking a shower when I get home. Preacher John has moved on from scripture to the eulogy. I glance around and spot Mary a couple rows back. She's fanning herself with a program and smiles at me. I smile back before facing the front again. Mary called me yesterday and told me Dr. Gregory has been calling into sick to work since the Mayor went missing and rumor has it Sally left town. I went by her apartment yesterday before yoga and no one answered the door. The curtains were drawn so I couldn't see inside. One of her neighbors said she hadn't seen her in a couple days.

I feel like I have all the pieces I need to solve this case except for the file in Vicky's office. I plan to sneak into the spa after the funeral. Bethany will be busy burying her mom and eating lunch so it will give me an opportunity to check out what's in the file. I wish I could get my hands on the information Sally had on April and the Mayor and of course me, but I have a feeling I won't be seeing it anytime soon. I'm kicking myself for not looking at it sooner. Of course, my life has been a little crazy lately...nothing like a few break-in's, murders, someone stalking and shooting at me, fighting with my BFF and reconnecting with Travis to keep me busy.

Preacher John continues to drone on about Vicky and that's when I see her. Sally. She's standing off to the side. The church is crowded so several people are standing. She's hiding behind on of the pillars. I almost didn't recognize her. She's dressed in black. Her hair isn't up in its usual bun, but cascading down her back. Tears are falling down her cheeks as she stares at Vicky's body. I tilt my head to the side to study her better. She seems really upset. Are those tears of grief or guilt?

"Who are you staring at?" Josh mutters beside me.

"Sally." I nod toward her.

He follows my gaze and frowns. "I thought she left town."

"Guess not."

"Why is she crying?"

"That's what I'm trying to figure out. She only knew Vicky for a month. We should be the ones bawling like babies."

Josh scoffs. "Thanks for making me feel bad. You know I don't cry in public."

I roll my eyes. "Me neither, but Vicky wasn't only our employer, she was our friend. Who was she to Sally?"

Bethany squeezes my hand and I turn toward her. "Will you and Josh go with me to the cemetery?"

Shoot. I was hoping to sneak over to the spa and grab the file while she was burying her mother. I know, not very compassionate, but I'm trying to find out who killed her mother. It's really for her benefit. "Of course." I squeeze her hand back. Guess I'll have to go later tonight.

Finally, Preacher John stops preaching and I'm only mildly drenched in spit. He invites everyone to the town hall for lunch while Bethany and I guess me and Josh bury her mom. We follow Preacher John and the pallbearers to the cemetery behind the church.

Luckily, the snow has stopped and the sun is shining. The temperature is in the 50's so the snow is melting. Gotta love the crazy Missouri weather. One day there's a snow storm and the next it's sunny and feeling like spring is upon us.

The walk to the grave site is clear. Bethany sniffles beside me and clings to my coat. I keep my arm wrapped around her for fear she'll collapse. The poor thing is beside herself. I can't imagine losing a parent.

Speaking of parents, my dad, you know my lawyer, he's been stuck in Oklahoma for a week due to bad weather. I guess they got ice and snow for several days straight. Yesterday, the roads were finally clear and he was going to be here by dinner time tonight, but decided to drive back to Florida once I assured him I was no longer a suspect. At least I'm pretty sure Travis no longer considers me a suspect. Dad was happy to hear it and was even happier to head back to warmer weather.

He's never liked the cold and only stayed in Missouri for my mom. Now she's in love with the beach so I don't think I'll ever get them to move back...unless I give them grandkids, so far that's not happening any time soon. I'm kind of bummed, not about not having kids although someday kids would be nice, but I was looking forward to seeing him even though I just saw him a couple weeks ago at Christmas. He promised they'd come for a visit in the spring so I have that to look forward to.

We stop next to the gravesite. Vicky's coffin is placed before us and Preacher John gives one last blessing. Bethany steps forward and places a white rose on top of the coffin. Something catches my eye in the distance. Sally. She's standing by the tree line, watching. I can't see her face; she's too far away. When Bethany steps back beside me and I take in her profile something clicks. Suddenly it's like dominos falling and I think I've solved the case. At least I hope so because the plan that's forming in my mind is crazy.

I let Preacher John escort Bethany to the town hall while

I stay back and talk to Josh. We trail behind them slowly. I want to ensure we're out of ear shot. Sally has disappeared, which is a shame because I would have loved to question her. "I need you to spread a rumor."

Josh cocks an eyebrow. "A rumor? Me?"

I cringe. Josh is not the best person to spread gossip. In fact, he doesn't gossip at all, but I need his help. "I think I figured out who killed Vicky."

"What about April?"

I give him a look. "I think we all know Vicky did it."

"Really? I thought we weren't sure. Opening another spa doesn't seem like a very strong motive."

I shake my head. "I think it was the straw that broke the camel's back."

"I don't follow."

I sigh. "I think Vicky snapped after years of dealing with April's family drama."

Josh looks at me like I have eight heads. "I don't understand."

I pat his arm. "I'll explain it later, but I need you to help me. Can you do it?"

"Of course. I would do anything for you." He bumps my hip with his and gives me his signature Josh smile.

I smile. There's my BFF I know and love. "I need you to start talking about the murder although I'm sure everyone will be whispering about it. Just interject yourself into the conversation and tell them I've figured out who killed Vicky and I'm headed to the spa to find proof right now."

He frowns. "You're going to the spa...alone."

I nod although I'm not totally convinced this is the smartest idea, but it has to be done. I square my shoulders and face him when we reach the Jeep. "We have to set a trap for the killer. It's the only way we'll know for sure they killed Vicky."

"And who killed Vicky?"

"I don't want to say until I know for sure."

"I don't like this, Autumn. I should go with you."

"Go with you where?"

"Travis." Shoot he's going to ruin my plan. I have to get rid of him yet he might be handy to have around if I end up getting myself in trouble. "I'm going to the spa to check on things. With all the snow and freezing temps, I want to make sure the pipes haven't frozen."

"I'll go with you."

"You don't have too."

"I insist." He gestures to his SUV behind us.

I cock an eyebrow and cross my arms over my chest. "Have you been waiting for me?"

He shrugs and smiles.

Josh scowls. "As much as I hate to include him, you need to tell him what you have planned."

I smack Josh on the arm.

Travis's eyes grow dark. "What do you have planned, Autumn?"

"Nothing." I avoid his eyes.

"Autumn," he growls.

"I'm going inside to get something to eat then I'll do what you ask, Autumn, but please be careful." He squeezes my shoulder and I meet his eyes.

They're filled with worry and something else I don't want to see...love. Is my best friend really in love with me? I must be reading into things. I shake my head as Josh heads inside.

"Best friends again?"

I meet Travis's eyes. "Always."

He nods. "If you say so."

I frown. I don't like not knowing where me and Josh stand. We've always been best friends. Nothing more and nothing less. I plan to keep it that way.

"So, what's your big plan?"

"Nothing." I shrug and unlock my Jeep. "I'm going to the spa to check on the pipes. Make sure everything is ok since we haven't been there in a few days."

He narrows his eyes. "You're lying."

"Never." I hold a hand to my heart as if he's insulted me.

"Autumn."

"That's my name, don't wear it out." I slip behind the wheel. "Now if you'll excuse me I want to check on the spa and come back for some lunch."

"Why don't you eat first and then check on the spa?" His crosses his arms over his chest and stands in front of the Jeep.

I need to think of an excuse quickly and God bless Mr. Higgins. "Have you seen the food line? It's almost to the door." I point to the door Mr. Higgins just exited so he could smoke a cigar.

Travis follows my gaze to the hall and sighs. "Fine. Go check the spa, but I'm coming with you."

Shoot. Things aren't going as planned. I could stomp on Josh's foot for saying something to Travis about my plan, but I don't have time. He's probably already talking to someone in line. "Fine."

Travis moves to get in the passenger side and I lock the doors. He knocks on the window when I start the engine.

My heart is beating wildly. He's the police, but I need to do this alone. I can't risk him spooking the killer. I turn up the radio as he knocks louder.

"Autumn, let me in."

I shake my head like I can't hear him as I pull out of the parking spot. I check the rearview mirror and he's chasing after me. When I turn on the main road, I see him jump into his SUV. This is not going as planned.

22

I creep through the woods behind the spa. I took the long way to throw off Travis. My cell phone has been ringing non-stop. I finally turned it off. I don't need Travis tracking me and ruining my plan. Hopefully, he thought I was using the spa as a cover for doing something else so he's not waiting for me.

I let out the breath I've been holding as I take in the empty parking lot. Good. He's not here. I unlock the back door. My hands are shaking and I'm pretty sure it's not from the cold. A noise inside the spa makes me pause.

"Be quiet. I told you this was a bad idea."

Sally. What's she doing here?

I let the back door shut quietly behind me and tiptoe into the spa. A light is on in one of the treatment rooms. What is going on? Something in my gut tells me to grab the folder and get the heck out of here, but the sleuth in me wants answers. I go to the office and retrieve the folder to ensure I'm on the right path. The folder has everything I'm looking for.

I tuck it under my arm and walk toward the treatment

room. My hands are shaking and my heart is beating rapidly in my chest. I may pass out from fear, but I have to know the truth. When I reach the massage room, I take in the room. The Mayor is sitting in the arm chair. Alive, but looking kind of pale. His gray hair is sticking up in different directions and he's still in his hospital gown. Dr. Gregory is sitting on the massage table in his white lab coat; he turns and glares at me. Sally's still in her funeral clothes and was pacing the massage room before I walked in. Now she's frozen, eyes darting around the room. "Care to explain, Sally?" I lean against the door frame.

"It's not what it looks like, Autumn. I swear."

I smirk. "It looks like you kidnapped the Mayor."

She bites her red lips. "Well sort of, but he came willingly. Someone was trying to kill him. We had to keep him safe...right, Dad?"

I jerk at the word. Not because I didn't know he was her dad, but I didn't know Sally knew. "You knew?"

She nods.

The Mayor gives me a weak smile. "You found the folder." He gestures to the file in my hand. "Where was it?"

"In Vicky's desk."

"I've been trying to find that file for weeks."

"So, you're the one who's been breaking into the spa?"

The Mayor shrugs. "That file could have ruined me. Now..." He looks over at Sally and smiles. "Now, it doesn't matter. The truth needs to come out. I've spent years hiding it and it's only caused trouble."

I frown. "Why didn't you just ask Vicky for it?"

He sighs. "She was furious at me. Refused to talk to me. See me."

"Why?"

"I knew about Sally before she did and I didn't tell her

about it. Sally wanted to meet her mother on her terms. I wanted to respect her wishes. When Vicky found out, she threatened to send everything to the paper. Ruin my reputation."

"It would ruin hers too."

He shakes his head. "I don't think she cared anymore. After my wife died, she became obsessed with finding Sally. When she found out I knew about Sally a whole year before telling her, she was furious. Wanted to hurt me like I hurt her all these years. My reputation is important to me and she knew it. I was going to tell everyone about Sally, but on my own terms not in some sort of front page news scandal."

I nod. "You followed me?"

He shrugs. "I wanted to see if you found the file."

"You broke into my Jeep, didn't you?"

He shrugs again. "The door was unlocked. I found the file Sally gave you. It had some incriminating things in it so I took it."

"What about the out of state plates?"

"I borrowed it from a friend." His eyes met Dr. Gregory's.

"Friend?"

"Dr. Gregory's father and I have been friends for years. He was always bragging about his brilliant fertility specialist son. So, when April was trying so hard to get pregnant, his father recommended she see him. Didn't think he'd get himself caught up with her."

Dr. Gregory hangs his head. "April was a mistake."

Sally crosses her arms and looks away.

The room falls silent for a moment. My thoughts are all over the place. "And Sally?"

The Mayor scrubs a hand over his face. "As you know from the file, Vicky and I had an affair. Once right after her husband died. She got pregnant. Bethany was only a few months old. Everyone thought Vicky was just having trouble getting rid of the baby weight. She gave birth in Chicago and we gave our daughter up for adoption. It killed Vicky to do it, but we knew it was for the best. This small town. I was married. She widowed. People would talk. Our businesses would suffer or worse. We did what we thought was best at the time. Then after my wife died, we started dating in secret and decided to find our daughter." He smiles at Sally who returns his smile. "I asked Dr. Gregory to keep an eye on her. Make sure she was okay. Never expected him to fall in love with her."

Sally blushes and Dr. Gregory smiles.

The Mayor continues, "Unfortunately, someone found out about Sally and started blackmailing me. I wasn't ready to go public with anything until Vicky met her so I paid them. They bled me dry. I even started using funds from the city to pay them. I suspected April of the blackmail."

"And you told Vicky your theory."

"Yes." The Mayor drops his head into his hands. "I know she killed April."

"Because she told you."

"No, she told me," Sally piped up. "She was furious April was planning to open another spa and between learning I was her daughter, April's snide comments about my massage techniques and the blackmail, she snapped. I was waiting for her in her office when she was asking you about April. I heard her stomp off, but thought she would come back in the office, but I heard the scrape of the knife against the sharpening block and the next thing I know Vicky...I mean my mom is coming in telling me she's taken care of all our problems."

I nod. My theory was correct, but I still can't believe it. Vicky murdering someone. She was so sweet, but I can understand protecting your family. "That aligns with what Cat told the police too. So, Vicky killed April. Who killed Vicky?"

"I did." A voice comes from behind me.

I turn to find Bethany holding a gun. It's shaking in her hands. Her eyes are wild and filled with tears. "Why'd you do it?"

Bethany snorts. "She lied to me. My whole life she's lied to me. I found that file when her secret compartment snagged my favorite scrub pants. The birth certificate, adoption papers, and a picture of him kissing my mother." She points the gun at the Mayor.

He cringes and drops his head. "I loved her, Bethany. Your mother was the love of my life. I was just too stupid to do anything about it."

"Shut up!" Bethany screams and tightens her grip on the gun.

My heart starts beating faster. Maybe it was a bad idea to lose Travis. Bethany could shoot us all and get out of town before we're found. "Bethany, please put down the gun. We're just talking there's no need to..."

"Be quiet, Autumn. You wanted to play detective and put the clues together, now it's my turn to talk. I know you figured out it was me at the gravesite. I saw it in your eyes when you looked at me. Only you don't know why I did it, right?"

I nod although I'm pretty sure I know why, but it's better to keep her talking so she doesn't start shooting. I send up a prayer Travis drives by the spa and sees her car or Josh comes to check on me.

Bethany turns back to the Mayor. "You didn't love my mother. You loved your status. Your money. Not her. We struggled. She worked so hard to build this spa for me. We almost lost it until I found the file. A way to black mail you into saving us."

The Mayor's head jerks up. "You're the one who's been blackmailing me."

She shrugs. "A girls gotta do what girls gotta do and I had to save this spa. My spa. Except it's not anymore, is it, Sally?"

Sally looks down at her hands as Bethany continues. "Mom planned to leave me the spa when she retired then she promises it to you," she sneers at Sally. "But only if you stay here and marry this guy." Bethany gestures to Dr. Gregory. "You all think you're so smart, but I'm the genius here. I have dirt on all of you." She sniffles again and narrows her eyes. "I know April found out about Sally and visited her in Chicago. She threatened you, right?"

Sally nods.

"But that didn't deter you, did it?" Bethany didn't let Sally speak before continuing. "You should have stayed in Chicago. Stayed away. Then I wouldn't have had to kill my own mother." Tears are running down Bethany's cheeks. "She was my best friend. We were partners. Then she found you and acted like I didn't exist."

"So, you smothered her?" Probably not the best choice of words, but I was shocked sweet Bethany killed her own mother.

"She wouldn't listen. Kept going on and on about Sally and how we could all run the spa together. I didn't want a sister. Never have. Never will." She sneers at Sally. "I only wanted her to be quiet. To listen to me, but she wouldn't. She just kept talking. I had to stop her from talking." Bethany's voice hitches and more tears spill from her eyes.

I want to reach out to comfort her and to try and take the gun from her, but I'm a little more than afraid of what she'll do. "Did you try and run me over and shoot the Mayor?"

Bethany sniffles. "You were snooping around. Making a list of suspects. Mom was getting worried so I thought if you saw Dr. Gregory's SUV, you would suspect him. I only wanted to scare you." She pauses and almost looks guilty for trying to run me over then turns to the Mayor. "This is all his fault. If it weren't for him, my mother would still be alive and so would April."

I frown. "So, you stole his SUV? Or I guess Dr. Gregory's SUV?"

Bethany nods again. "His SUV was parked behind the church at April's funeral. Keys were in the ignition. I took it, tried to scare you then did a loop around the park and parked it back where it was. No one saw me. The Mayor was still in the town hall eating lunch." She pauses again and tightens her grip on the gun. "He parked in the same spot when he went to visit April's grave. I took it, shot at him then when Travis was chasing me, I parked it in my garage. No one suspected me until you decided to play detective." She turns the gun on me. "I could have gotten away with everything. If only you would have kept your nose out of it. I'll be sure to comfort Josh for you."

An image of Bethany comforting Josh at my funeral flashes through my mind. My stomach turns as Bethany cocks the gun. "I'm sorry, Autumn. I really liked you."

My heart pounds in my chest. I know I only have a few seconds before I'm dead. Everyone in the room is frozen then the next thing I know Bethany is on the floor. Travis is knocking her to the ground and reading her the Miranda rights. Josh rushes in and takes me into his arms. I don't realize I'm shaking until he wraps his jacket around me and holds me to his chest. I breathe in his mint and tea tree scent. This time it does calm me as I watch everything go on around me.

Officers swarm the room. Asking questions. Taking statements. EMT's rush in and insist on taking a pale looking Mayor back to the hospital. Dr. Gregory wraps an arm around a crying Sally and follows the EMT's. Travis has an officer escort them and I heard something about them needing to obtain a lawyer. I hope Sally isn't in too much trouble. She's a sweet girl not to mention my new boss.

Travis's eyes meet mine and by the way his jaw clenches, I can tell he doesn't like Josh comforting me, but right now I don't care. I want someone familiar. Someone who knows me and loves me unconditionally. Someone who hasn't betrayed me.

"Autumn, I need to get your statement." He rakes a hand through his hair.

I nod, but Josh interrupts, "Not now. I'm taking her home."

Travis opens his mouth to object, but then closes it. "I'll come by later to get it."

Josh places an arm around my shoulder and leads me toward the exit. My mind is still reeling with everything that's happened. Who would have thought so much deception would happen in the small town of Daysville? An affair, a baby, blackmail, stalking, murder, attempted murder. It seems like this is all a bad dream. I yawn. The day has definitely taken a toll on me.

Snow is falling again and the temperature has dropped. When we get inside my Jeep, Josh turns to me with tears in his eyes and grabs my hand. "I almost lost you. Don't ever do that to me again. You almost gave me a heart attack." His tone was gruff, but I could tell he was really just worried.

I can't blame him. Staring down the barrel of a gun was

nothing I care to repeat. My whole life flashed before my eyes and made me realize some things need to change.

I squeeze his hand. "I'm glad you came when you did. What took you so long?"

Josh shakes his head. "I was talking to Mary when I noticed Bethany was gone. She was sitting next to me as I was going on about how you solved the murders and was collecting evidence right now to prove it. First, I thought she went to the bathroom, but when she didn't come back in a few minutes, I checked the parking lot. Her car was gone. Travis pulled up and said you purposely lost him. I told him your ridiculous plan and we hightailed it over here."

I scoff. "It wasn't a ridiculous plan. Bethany would have gotten away with murder."

"But you could have been killed."

"But I wasn't."

Josh growls. "Promise me this is the last case you will ever stick your nose into."

I take in my best friend. He's upset. Worried. I get it, but he'll get over it. Sleuthing is in my blood just like massage. It's not something I can just give up, but I give him my best smile, tuck my crossed fingers underneath my leg and say, "I promise."

A NOTE FROM THE AUTHOR

Thank you so much for reading this book! I so appreciate your support.

I've been a Licensed Massage Therapist since 2003. A long time, I know. This story came to me while I was talking with a client one day. She has a friend who is a yoga instructor and she started a cozy mystery series about a yoga instructor who solves mysteries. What a great idea! Surely, a massage therapist can be a sleuth, right?

I absolutely love Autumn and I hope you do too. Her wit and charm just kind of flowed out of me and the small town of Daysville has me wanting to start my own little town in Missouri. Josh is my favorite male character at the moment. Travis hasn't quite redeemed himself in my eyes yet, but maybe he'll get there. I'm eager to start working on the next book, "Hot Stones & Homicides." Josh will find himself in a bit of a predicament and who will be there to help him out? You guessed it, our beloved Autumn. Surely, Josh will forget he asked her to stop sleuthing when he's in the hot seat, right? Be sure to keep an eye out for it.

Writing a book is a commitment and not something that

can be done alone. I have a few people to thank for helping with this book.

Mariah Sinclair is the queen of Cozy Mystery Covers and I absolutely adore this cover. Her work is incredible and I'm so thankful for her creative vision on this cover.

I would also like to give a huge shout out to Kelly for being my eyes on this book. Helping me spot plot holes, punctuation errors and ensuring this book is flawless for you to enjoy.

My family is also amazing. Shouting out character names when I need one, bringing me food and drinks when I'm busy typing away and just encouraging me to follow my dreams. Without them, I would struggle. They're my rocks and I love them dearly.

Another huge thank you to you, my reader, I so appreciate you and your support. If you would like to follow me on social media or check out my blog. Here are the links:

Sleuth Mama Website (Blog)

Facebook Instagram Twitter Pinterest

ABOUT THE AUTHOR

Jenn Cowan is the author of several genres and pen names under Jenna Richert and J.R. Cowan. When she's not writing you can find her in her massage office working on clients, cooking up a storm in her kitchen, hitting her yoga mat, singing and dancing with her hubby at a concert, cheering on the sidelines for her kiddos or cozied up by the fire reading a novel. She loves a good mystery and a happily ever after.

OTHER BOOKS BY THE AUTHOR:

Massage Basics: A Step By Step Guide to At Home Massage

Love at the Manor

Fate at the Manor

Made in the USA
Middletown, DE
28 March 2018